PRAISE FOR NOELLE RAHN-JOHNSON

5 Stars for In Pieces

"Wow!!! What a good book. It's very addictive."

— Paula Genereau, Goodreads

4 Stars for In Pieces

"IN PIECES is a brilliant work of emotion.
Noelle Rahn-Johnson brings her characters to life
by showing the reader every emotion on the
spectrum and weaving it throughout a sweet
story. This book will make you laugh and cry.
From page 1, the reader is pulled in and made to
feel as if she lives right along beside Paige,
cheering Paige's triumphs as well as offering a
shoulder for Paige to cry on. I cannot wait to see
where Noelle Rahn-Johnson takes me next!"

— Allie Harrison, Goodreads

PRAISE FOR NOELLE RAHN-JOHNSON

5 Stars for Shattered Pieces

"This is he best love story I've read in a while. I love Colton and Betsey's story. Betsey's and Colton are best friends but at their friends wedding something happens that could be more or ruin their friendship."

— Paula Genereau, Goodreads

4 Stars for Shattered Pieces

"I'm going to come right out and say it. I haven't really been a big fan of the contemporary romance genre for quite a while. I suppose it is because in many cases, the books have such shallow characters that it's just no fun to read the books. But that certainly is not the case with Shattered Pieces."

— Charli, Goodreads

PRAISE FOR NOELLE RAHN-JOHNSON

5 Stars for In Pieces

"In Pieces is an amazing read by a great author. The chemistry just crackles between Ronan and Paige. She is afraid of the relationship because of things that happened in her past so she tries to keep it at arms length. Ronan isn't going to give up!"

— Heather Swan, Amazon Reader

5 Stars for Returning for Ryder

"A beautiful story about finding out who Ryder really is. The emotional journey he takes and the loving support he has really helps him along with what he finds out. Flynn has known he he loves for a very long time but he has to wait for that person to grow more. Due to circumstances he comes home to calm his love but he's uncertain if it will be returned."

— Jeanette Kelley, Amazon Reader

PRAISE FOR NOELLE RAHN-JOHNSON

5 Stars for Shattered Pieces

"This book had me on edge the whole way!
Emotionally I can relate with all characters of the
story and I feel like I am living it with them, like
I was meant to be part of it!"

— Cheryl, Goodreads

5 Stars for In Pieces

"Emotional roller coaster!!
I don't think I have read a book lately that I
wanted to scream, cry and smack the main
characters so much! Paige is a young adult going
through too many life breaking events for her to
handle as she meets Ronan, the man is sexy as
hell, and she feels inadequate. The strongest love
lives through everything that is built to tear it
down..."

— Bookworm, Amazon Reader

PRAISE FOR NOELLE RAHN-JOHNSON

5 Stars for Returning for Ryder

"Oh My God! What an awesome book!
I loved the Story of Ryder and Flynn! Made want
to hug them both I was so happy for them. Now I
can't wait for Chances story! Well written and
very well put together to bring these two men to
light! An Exciting story."

— Amazon Customer

5 Stars for Broken Pieces

"Final book to the series blew me away!
Hayden and Cece's story was beautifully written
of two people who had no clue that growing up in
each other's lives from second grade to adulthood
would end up with each other. Business partners
and bestfriends find out they are madly in love
with each other. You must read this series."

— Amazon Customer

PRAISE FOR NOELLE RAHN-JOHNSON

5 Stars for Shattered Pieces

"I loved this book!

The story of Colton and Betsy Ann's love story is beautifully written. The ups and downs keep you wanting more! And the cliffhanger brings you to your knees screaming noooooooo! But book three is out and you can get right back into it! A must read! This author writes from the heart you will love her work!

— Amazon Customer

5 Stars for In Pieces

"Fast read, realistic story.

I definitely will read the next book in the series!"

— Wanda, Amazon Customer

Remote in the Shadows

Second Edition

Dedication

For...

Terold Erwin Rahn, my daddy. Who passed away
November 20th, 2007.

He has inspired me in all my writing.

My hubby, *Gary Johnson*, for surviving this year
with me of complaints, his patience, and for
always believing in me and holding my hand
along the way.

My kids, for just being you.

My daughter, *Cheyenne*, for helping me pick out
music and with helping with a few issues in the
book, and thinks she should be the first one
mentioned...

My *mom and grandma*, for wanting the books!

Acknowledgements

To my beta readers for this book: *Heather Swan* and *Phyllis Lopez* thanks for being there and reading this book. Glad you both loved it! Sorry for putting Heather through agony every five minutes while writing the last one hundred pages and have her wait for the final ending. Thanks to the both of you for being such great friends and demanding more books from me!

To *Gina*, for the pushing me to get it done, being a friend, and for believing in me. And, for cracking the whip. *Snap!*

To *Willsin Rowe*, for making me an absolutely beautiful cover.

Of course, a huge thanks goes out to my *incredible faithful readers, fans, and friends*—too many to name—you are the reason I push myself to write every day.

Music Line Up for Remote in the Shadows

Song and Artist Credits

Blood on my Hands -- Through fire

Blush (Only You) -- Plumb

Animal I have Become -- 3 Days Grace

Breathe Me -- Sia

Bully -- Shinedown

Alive -- Sia

Titanium -- David Guetta & Sia

Follow You -- Bring me the Horizon

Feel Invincible -- Skillet

Breathe (Extended Version) -- Through Fire

Taking you Down -- Egypt Central

Unbreakable -- Firelight

Wrapped up in your Arms -- Firelight

Back for More -- Five Finger Death Punch

Chasing Cars -- Snow Patrol

I am the Fire -- Halestorm

Remote in the Shadows

Noelle Rahn-Johnson

Chapter One

THE BLUISH BLACK of the night sky overhead, still hangs heavy. The last of the stars twinkling out as a faint light begins to peek over the horizon. The dew is heavy on the forest floor, the light rains from the night before still coat the leaves of the trees with a musty wood scent.

At twenty-seven, Parker James Williams lives alone in a two-story log cabin home in the wilderness, in a remote part of Oregon. This is where his ancestors settled many, many years ago. This is where he prefers to stay, where it's safe from civilization, he can hunt, frolic and run the forest without fear of discovery. This is his element and he lives in it as naturally as one would when their animal form is a midnight black leopard.

It's the first week of June, and it's starting to warm up during the daytime hours. So, Parker takes his liberties and hunts early in the mornings, before daylight. All the little creatures are still roaming and scavenging for their own pre- daybreak meals.

He's crouched behind a large fallen branch, stalking a fawn and two white-tailed does. Suddenly, when the wind shifts, he smells blood. *Human blood.* He's momentarily confused by the ridiculous thought that he could scent human's way out here in the uncultivated wilderness. His leopard instinctively hisses and steps backwards a pace, and steps on an eroded, stray stick. It makes a crunching sound and sends his dinner scurrying off into the deep brush. Cursing himself for his momentary lapse of judgment, he gives his massive head a shake, as if to eliminate the last shred of doubt from his mind. Even his stomach chastises him with a loud rumble of displeasure. Letting out a long, low growl, Parker paws the ground, his claws scratching the leaves and dirt in four long marks. With a last sniff to the wind, he sets off to mark his next potential serving of food. And to find out where this human blood is coming from.

His heavy paws squish into the earth and mud. He's running through the heavily wooded forest when an odd sound reaches through the feral brain of his beast and registers within the human at its core – the faint cry of a small child in the distance.

Cresting a ridge, Parker comes to a stop. He scours the land with the keen night vision of his animal, and he catches a flash of a tan colored mass resting mid-way down an embankment across the gorge from where he stands. It's a steep drop from the rarely used, paved service road through these hills near his home. The driver must have been lost to have taken this road. In fact, in the many years he's been living here, he's the only one to drive that road, that he knows of. Not even emergency vehicles or the rangers bother to use it in favor of the newly paved single lane highway fifteen miles back that ends in the same small, beaten down town.

His sensitive ears can hear a soft whimpering sound from inside of the mangled tan car. It registers in his brain somehow that these sounds come from an infant.

Wondering why anyone would be out in this remote location on such a beaten track to begin with, strikes him as odd. But who in their right mind would be out this early and driving it in the dark of all things.

He creeps up to the side of the vehicle, the pads of his feet not making a sound on the loose earth. He notices the front end of the vehicle compressed into a tree, saving it from tumbling the rest of the way down the steep hill. His keen nose picks up the scent of radiator fluid, once again mixed with the unmistakable copper aroma of blood. Hearing a hissing noise coming from the front of the vehicle where it has combined with the tree, his nose was correct on the car spewing its contents all over the floor of the forest. Great, that aught to attract the porcupines and other small rodent type creatures he hates so much. Why they like the taste and smell of coolant and brake fluid, he will never understand. With a sigh at the uselessness of such inedible animals, Parker moves up to peer into the glass of the back window, seeing the first rays of dawn creeping up over his shoulder in the reflection. Wet nose pressed against the glass now, he can see there's a young toddler strapped into a car seat, unmoving except for a light rise and fall of her little chest underneath the taunt straps. The scent of blood is stronger here, but it's not coming from her.

The driver's side window has been smashed out, either from the impact to the tree or the car roughly rolling down the embankment. Parker pokes his thick head into the opening, careful not to catch his fur on the remaining shards. A woman is leaning back against her seat, still belted in and unconscious. She has a deep gash above her left eyebrow and there's still a trickle of fresh bright red blood running down her forehead to her chin. He draws a deep breath in through his nose, identifying this as the human blood he'd first smelled when he was about to pounce on his dinner. The woman is still alive. For now, anyway.

The woman is miles from any clinic or hospital and the child seems unharmed, though perhaps the whimpers are of fear or hunger. At this point it's impossible to assess the situation further in his leopard form. Not only because he can't possibly open the doors with his big furry paws, but also because the last thing he needs right now is a screaming woman if she wakes and catches sight of some big cat in her face. If he shifts here, though, he'll be naked and that's pretty likely to send her off into hysterics as well.

Hating to leave them alone but determining there's no immediate danger anywhere in the vicinity and the car, though damaged pretty bad, doesn't seem like it's going anywhere being wedged against the tree the way it is. There's no spark, and frankly barely any heat left to the ticking engine and radiator, and he feels fairly confident the child is unharmed. With the woman only having the slightly bleeding wound on her head, he hopes he's right and can leave them behind in the current safety of the car.

He's going to have to take a chance and make a run home for some clothing and bring back his truck.

Parker gives one last sniff of the open window and takes off running full out for home.

Chapter Two

Upon returning to the woman and child, Parker slowly slides down the embankment on his heels, leaving his 4X4 truck running, headlights on high beams. Really, it's only on the rare chance any other vehicles are actually driving the windy paved road. His cat can see perfectly at night, even in his human form.

He opens the back door of the damaged vehicle, then unbuckles the seat belt from around the baby's car seat, slowly lifting the carrier from the back of the car.

He notices a backpack on the floor and grabs it. Tossing the backpack strap over his shoulder, he takes the quiet sleeping baby, still strapped inside of the carrier, up to his truck; losing footing occasionally on the steep embankment.

Parker buckles the carrier into the back seat of his truck and sets the backpack on the floor. Pausing for a moment to watch the rise and fall of the child's chest as she breathes, clearly in a deep sleep despite the trauma of the accident, he then closes the truck door with a small snick sound.

Parker makes his way back down to the woman, sliding down on his ass despite the mud and debris he knows is probably ruining his pants. Moving to the driver's door, he can smell her blood wafting through the broken window.

Opening the door, he leans in carefully over the woman, and grabs the keys from the ignition, shoving them into his pocket. He unbuckles the seatbelt from around her, careful not to let the strap injure her further.

Parker puts his arm out in front of her chest, catching her as she moans and slumps forward slightly.

He slides one hand under her legs and the other one behind her shoulders very gently, pulling her from the car and into his arms. He's careful to cradle her head against his shoulder, not wanting to hurt her any more than she already is. She fits easily against his chest. Parker can hear his leopard purring in contentment inside his head.

What are you purring about? It's a woman, she's hurt and needs help, that's all. Parker chastises his beast.

I like her. She's going to be ours soon. The inner cat purrs back.

Knock it off. She is not. Parker replies.

As he carries the woman, being careful of his footing, he slowly makes it back up the hill. He places her inside the truck and buckles her in. He flashes a quick glance in the backseat and breathes a sigh of relief that the child is still asleep.

Sliding down the embankment one more time, he checks the vehicle over for anything the woman or the baby may need and finds the woman's purse on the floor of the passenger side. He opens the trunk and finds a suitcase and a box of diapers.

Grabbing everything, Parker carries all of it up the side of the hill. He puts everything in the back seat behind the woman, checking the baby once again and shuts the door quietly.

Parker then climbs into the driver's seat and puts the truck in drive after clicking in his own seatbelt. On the way home, Parker's mind is racing. *Why would a woman take a small child out in the middle of the night with suitcases unless she was running or hiding from someone? Or maybe she's traveling and knows the child would sleep better at night?*

Not ten minutes later, they arrive at Parker's home and he parks the vehicle next to the front entrance. He gets out and unbuckles the baby's car seat, throws the backpack and the purse over his shoulder, grasps the baby carrier in one meaty hand, and walks through the front door to the large four-bedroom home.

Carefully setting the baby carrier on the floor in the master bedroom, he sets the purse and backpack on the floor by the dresser.

Returning to the truck, he grabs the box of diapers and the suitcase, and puts them next to the other bags in the master bedroom.

Returning one last time for the woman, noticing that her eyes are still closed, he carefully lifts her from the passenger seat and shuts the truck door. Lifting her is easy. He's extremely fit because of his nature. He's a leopard and he runs nightly on his one thousand acres of wilderness.

Pulling the blankets back, he gently lays the injured woman down on the bed. He then takes off her tennis shoes and socks, trying not to disturb her. Then he sets them on the floor next to the bed.

Covering up the woman with the blanket to her shoulders, Parker goes back to the living room and grabs the small throw blanket off the back of the couch for the baby.

Moving the car seat next to the bed so when the woman wakes up, she can see that her baby is safe, he lightly drapes the throw over the child's lower half, careful to make sure it's tucked snug in the carrier straps so the child won't get tangled in it if she should wake. He flicks the small light on next to the bed, just in case this beautiful woman wakes up scared in this unfamiliar place.

Noticing her hair is now sticking to the dried blood on her forehead, he lightly runs his hand across her temple, pushing the errant hairs away from the cut as his inner cat growls at the sight.

With the soft glow from the lamp, he notices a nasty bruise surrounding her right eye and her left cheek is colored, as well. It's reddened from what it looks like a handprint. He carefully checks her arms for any other bruising and sees fingermark bruising on her biceps.

Parker doesn't see a wedding ring on her ring finger, so maybe it's from a boyfriend. The idea makes his cat growl deeper, wondering how anyone could harm such intense beauty.

She has dark blonde hair, small pouty lips, and a thin straight nose. She's short, just a little more than five feet tall, and weighs around one hundred and thirty pounds or so. Only by judging by how she felt in his arms, with a smaller body frame, but a fuller figure in the middle, hips, and ass. A real looking woman, not the stick figures trying to keep that hourglass shape. Just what Parker likes in his woman.

Wait. What? His woman?

Dammit! He knows he's not allowed to feel this way. He had his chance. He lost his mate. There is only one soul mate for every leopard, and his is gone.

Parker's wife, Hailey, died six years ago and his chance for a mate along with her. He still carries the guilt from the death of her and their unborn baby girl, Emily May.

Parker and Hailey had argued that morning, and she left to go for a walk. He doesn't even remember what the argument was about anymore. It wasn't a major argument but when Hailey got riled up over something, her badger animal came out and she easily lost her temper. He thought it was cute sometimes to watch her heat up.

Her face would turn pink, her lips reddening and becoming fuller. Her stance, her strength, her beauty showing even more as she'd square her shoulders, straighten her back, and prepare to give him holy hell before stomping out the door. It made for great make up sex.

That day Parker had felt the pain through their shifter connection and he ran as fast as he could to find her. He knew she liked to go walking in the woods on the well-worn path every day to clear her head and think privately. He always let her have that time, something he'd live to regret.

She was seven months pregnant when she fell in the woods, tripping over a root peeking out from the leaf litter.

She hit her belly first, then hit her head as she slammed into the ground with no protection.

When Parker found Hailey, her head was bleeding, and she was lying flat on her stomach. She was unresponsive when he screamed out her name. He quickly and carefully lifted her into his arms, noticing blood pooling under her and between her legs as well. He ran as fast as his human legs could carry her.

Despite getting her home and calling the doctor as fast as he could, there was nothing Parker could have done for her. Hailey died from her head injuries, they were too severe for her shifter to heal. Their unborn daughter was too early to survive. The hemorrhaging was uncontrollable.

Six years of uncontrollable agony. Six years of self-blame and depression. Six years of being alone to think of nothing but her. Six years living with self-recrimination, knowing her dying was all his fault. He wasn't fast enough to save her or the baby.

Giving himself a mental shake from the memories filling his mind, Parker turns his attention back to the woman in the bed.

Nothing like Hailey. And a human. She could handle the mating. We need someone who has meat on her. Shifters mating with humans is different than it is with shifters mating with other shifters. Parker's leopard whispers in his head.

I said to shut up. She's not doing any mating. With anyone. Parker pushes the last thought out with more conviction.

Parker's inner cat growls and then ends up purring. He likes this woman, a lot. He's pushing images of Parker and the woman in the throes of mating passion through Parker's mind.

"Stop it!" Parker growls out loud and the woman stirs. The baby remains unmoving.

He walks quietly out of the bedroom, brooding and confused. Closing the door behind him, he stomps up the stairs to the second floor. He makes his way down the hall and into the smallest bedroom. He quickly strips out of his clothes and shoes, then walks back down the hall, naked, to the bathroom at the end of the hallway.

Turning on the shower, leaving the bathroom door open, Parker quickly gets under the spray of water. He soaps and tries to ignore where his inner cat's earlier thoughts were taking him.

After a quick wash in the shower, he dries off quickly and pads back to the smaller bedroom, still naked. Parker climbs into the small full-size bed and falls asleep, his mind filled with thoughts of his new temporary roommates.

Parker wakes up to soft cries. He jumps up out of bed and quickly slides on a pair of jeans and pulls a tee shirt over his head. It's only been a few hours since he climbed into bed after he rescued the woman and her baby. He runs down the steps to the main floor, not knowing what he'll find.

Is the woman still unconscious? Is the baby in need of something and is the mother not hearing her cry? He's fully prepared to care for the child until the woman is well again.

Parker stops outside of the master bedroom door. The soft muffled cries have now stopped. He listens closely at the door and he can hear the woman inside softly crooning the young child back to sleep.

Walking into the kitchen, Parker starts the coffee maker to brew a full pot. At least he could start a late breakfast, consisting of fried potatoes, bacon, scrambled eggs and toast.

Not knowing what the woman likes or what to feed the child, Parker works over the food and plates up everything. He sets the plates in the warmer then walks back to the master bedroom. He stops outside the door, listens for a moment and then knocks quietly. No answer.

He knocks again a little louder and can hear movement from inside now. He doesn't want to frighten the woman but wants to at least let her know she's not in any danger. Her or her child.

"Ma'am, I'm sorry to disturb you. But I wanted to let you know I've made breakfast. It's in the warmer when you're ready. I'll be waiting in the kitchen. I'm not going to hurt you or your baby, but I'd like to talk to you. Please." He calls quietly but is firm on what he wants.

He leaves it at that, walking back to the kitchen and sits at the table with his own plate of food, coffee and a fork. As he's eating, he can hear feet shuffling. Down the hallway, a door creaks open then closes. Footsteps and then another door closes.

Silence.

Parker hears the door open again about fifteen minutes later and then a face appears around the corner of the kitchen entrance.

The woman has washed her face free of the blood and changed her clothes from the night before. No baby, so she must have left her in the bedroom.

She comes out from behind the door frame and Parker stays seated so as not to scare her. He gestures to the chair across from him for her to sit down. When she does, Parker slowly gets up and grabs her plate of food from the warmer and places it in front of her.

"Would you like some coffee? I just made it." Parker asks her softly.

"Yes, please." She says quietly while staring at her plate, not eating yet and not making eye contact with him. She's hiding behind the thick curtain of her hair.

A timid little bird. She needs to gain strength and confidence in herself. Someone has emotionally beat this woman down. Parker's not used to someone not talking to him. He's a bit of a loner but still craves human contact. He'll need to get her to open up to him. For her and him both.

He sets down a cup of hot coffee and places the milk and sugar next to her as well. She uses both and he pays attention to what she uses.

"Thank you." She says nervously, still not making eye contact with him. She slowly starts to eat her breakfast after he sits down and then he finishes his.

"What's your name?" Parker asks quietly.

"Addison. Addison Grace Smithers. My daughter's name is London." She whispers, still with her head down and eating.

"Well, Addison. My name is Parker. Parker James Williams, and this is my home. I found you unconscious in your car a few miles from here, and your little girl was crying in the back seat. I grabbed your purse, backpack, a box of diapers, and a suitcase from your vehicle and brought you both here. I have your keys on the counter."

She nods and says, "Thank you, Parker. When I'm done here, I'll grab our things and we'll be on our way. I don't want to bother you or your family." She glances up to meet Parker's eyes.

She has the most beautiful mossy green eyes he's ever seen.

Her long, flowing hair is down and glossy from just being brushed out, and it hides her face from him.

"Addison, neither one of you are a bother to me and I live here alone. You were hurt, and I couldn't leave you in your wrecked vehicle with a baby. You're safe here, from whomever you're running from."

She looks at Parker with panic in her eyes and gets up from her chair. Quickly walking with the half empty plate and setting it on the counter by the sink, she walks swiftly to the bedroom, shutting the door behind her quietly.

Shit. What did he say to upset her? He sets his plate on the counter next to hers and walks to her closed bedroom door. Parker raps softly with his knuckles and says, "Addison, I'm sorry I upset you. I don't know what I said to hurt you. Please, come back out so I can help you."

He realizes he's so out of his element here. Hailey, his deceased wife was outgoing, outspoken, and so full of life, while Addison is so closed off, timid, and quiet. Two totally different women, and yet, the same. Parker checks the doorknob and tries to turn it, finding she locked it.

"Addison, please open the door. I'm not going to hurt you." Parker leans his forehead against the door and listens to the quiet sounds on the other side. Muffled crying, like she has a pillow stuffed to her face to be quiet.

Damn. He made her cry. He doesn't handle women crying very well. In this case, he made her cry and he needs to fix this. He rattles the doorknob and hears Addison scream out in fear.

"Addison, I'm sorry. I didn't mean to scare you. Can you please come and unlock the door? I need to talk to you." He backs away from the door with both hands up in surrender. He doesn't know how else to handle this but with slow and quiet movements.

You need to make sure she's okay. I can't sit here and not know if she's safe. Parker's leopard growls within his head and he can feel his unease; like he's pacing within the walls of his own skull.

She's safe if she's here with us. Whoever beat her and made her this afraid will pay. With their life, I swear on it. Parker growls back.

Hearing Addison shuffle across the floor, the lock clicks open. "Addison? Is it okay if I open the door?" He asks her, wanting to make sure.

"Yes." She says quietly.

"I'm so sorry. I didn't mean to upset you." Parker tells her while opening the door cautiously. She's sitting on the bed in a flash, and is leaning against the headboard, her knees up to her chest, her arms wrapped around her legs pulling them in tightly. She's making herself look smaller. She's trying to hide.

The baby's still asleep but on the bed with pillows around her. A makeshift crib. Parker gestures to the foot of the bed, asking silently if he can sit there.

She nods her head yes.

This is a start.

He moves to sit down next to her on the bed, noticing her flinch just slightly, and all he wants to do is pull her to him, hold her until she feels safe. He can see she's afraid and it only makes him want to protect her from the demons haunting her, making her want to run and hide.

Parker looks over to London; she stirs next to them then rolls over onto her stomach. He watches in awe as she lifts her head off the soft blanket and opens her light blue eyes. She looks at her momma and then at Parker. She smiles, and he sees dimples in both chubby cheeks.

The baby giggles and he can't help but smile at her cuteness. Baby London scooches up on her hands and knees and then sits on her butt, rubbing her eyes and yawns. She looks back at Parker and looks him over. He smiles and wiggles his fingers at her. She smiles, giggling and clapping her hands together.

Parker looks back at Addison and she's still pulled together tightly, and it pains him to see her this way. "Addison, can you tell me what I did to scare you away to hide in here?"

He can see tears glistening in the corners of her eyes and one falls over, sliding down over her cheek.

She hides her face in her arms.

He scoots closer, wanting to touch her, but knowing better. He hasn't earned the right to touch her without her permission.

Addison glances up at him through lowered lashes, clearly nervous and afraid that he's come so close to her. Her eyes are red and puffy, and her cheeks tear streaked. She's battling inner demons and he wants her to trust him. He *needs* to have her trust in him, but how?

Give her time. The leopard whispers, sensing Parker's unease.

Parker hates that his feline is right. He lifts his hand to rest it on her knee, but she flinches before he can do so. He did it without even thinking about it. He's now convinced she's been abused, hit, smacked around, just from her reaction. Sighing, he leans back, shaking his head slightly.

"Addison, I won't hurt you. I promise. You two are safe here in my home with me." He's repeating himself, but he wants her to open to him, to tell him what's happened to her in the past. Baby London seems to be okay. She's a happy baby and is sucking on her fingers, drooling.

"I have to feed her; do you have any milk in your fridge? Or eggs?" She asks him, dodging his questions.

Not knowing what else London can eat, he asks her, "Why don't you make a list of what you two need and I can drive us into town later."

"I have some money. I took it when I packed our clothes. I can help. She's my baby. I can care for her. I'm not some charity case or someone who needs your pity." Determined, she sits up and drops her feet to the floor.

She stands up and turns around to pick up London. Before she's able to grab her, Parker reaches out to her hand. Their skin touches and his skin burns where she touches him. Not painful, but like a tingling, zing. An electric shock or something.

Ours. Parker's inner cat growls.

The closeness of Addison and him, her legs right next to his, an inch or so separating their bodies, is intoxicating. Parker brings his right knee up on the bed, so he can angle towards her better. He pulls her wrist closer and she stumbles that last inch, her thigh now touching his. The only thing separating their skin is the jeans they're both wearing. His breath hitches and he rubs his thumb across the soft skin at her wrist.

She pulls her hand away from him a few seconds later. "Please, don't touch me again. I don't like to be touched."

Parker wonders if he should ask why, but before he can, Addison picks London up from the bed and sets her on her hip, then walks out into the kitchen. He follows her, watching her backside sway from side to side. He can feel himself harden slightly under his jeans.

He's always loved the way a woman walks. Watching her body move. The softer side of a woman and the softness of her curves, fitting with his muscular body.

When he's out in his leopard form, he runs, leaps, pulls and pushes his body hard. It keeps him active, fit, strong and limber.

Parker follows her out to the living room and she sets London on the floor. She goes back into her room and grabs a diaper, clothes, and little shoes along with a small mesh bag with some toys in it. Addison sits on the living room floor and starts to change London.

Parker watches her as she changes and clothes the baby with such tender care, mumbling soft words the entire time, and after London's all dressed, and her diaper is changed, Addison lets her crawl around. She grabs a few toys from the bag and sets them by London, setting the bag on the coffee table. Then Addison comes into the kitchen with Parker following behind her.

She opens the fridge, making herself at home, and pulls out eggs, butter, and milk. She searches the kitchen looking for what else she needs and starts breakfast for London.

"Oh, damn," she whispers. "Can I ask you to go into my backpack on the floor in the bedroom and grab a bottle from inside, so I can give her some milk, please?" Addison asks him, her voice still very light and timid.

"Sure." Parker walks into her room and finds the backpack. Lifting it up to the bed, he unzips the main compartment. He finds the bottle pushed over on the far side and when he pulls it out, he notices a lot of money underneath.

He fingers the bills and he thinks she must have around five hundred dollars in cash. She's running, but why and from whom? Parker pushes the money back down and zips the bag closed. He then sets it back where he found it.

Walking back out to the kitchen, he unscrews the bottle top and hands it to Addison. She fills it with milk for London, then hands the baby the bottle.

No conversation occurs between the two of them and Parker's getting uncomfortable. Watching her, it's like she knows her way around his kitchen and she's finding things easily.

He finally sits down at the kitchen table and watches her make London's breakfast, sipping his coffee. "So, are we going to talk, or do I get to sit here and watch you cook?"

"Sorry. I'm not a talker. I'm kind of a quiet and shy person. I've been told to be quiet, that I have a nauseating voice." She looks back to the stove, "Me, here in your kitchen, this is me talking. I love to cook." She looks back over her shoulder and gives him a shy smile.

There is nothing wrong with her voice. It's beautiful, and Parker wants to hear more from her. "If you're here, I want to know you, know your daughter. You're welcome to stay here for as long as you need to be. I obviously have the room." He chuckles.

He knows she's not a quiet person, because when she does talk to him, it's not one or two-word answers. She's been told to be quiet and that she doesn't matter. That's so wrong, she matters, all too much.

London crawls over to Parker and grabs the pant leg of his jeans, pulling herself up to standing. She wobbles a bit until she can balance and then let's go, clapping her hands together.

Then two seconds later, she plops down on her diapered butt and pouts.

Addison claps and praises her daughter and London claps some more. Parker laughs, and Addison goes back to cooking. She looks like she's in deep thought, her eyebrows pinched together.

"What's bothering you? I can see that you're thinking about something. Just tell me." Parker asks her as she sits down with the eggs, and feeds London from the plate with her fingers.

"I don't trust easily. And with my daughter with me, it's even harder. We've been taken advantage of too much lately and I just got us out of some trouble." She says the last part with anger inflected in her voice and a fake, small smile on her mouth.

"Well, I can understand that. I hope you can trust me and know I won't hurt either of you in any way. I hope you can trust me one day with who you're running from." Parker gets up and puts the dishes she used to cook with and his own from earlier in the dishwasher.

"Thank you for the conversation. I have some business to take care of in town this morning and I'll be back later for a shower, then we can go into town for groceries. If you can have a list ready by then, that would be great. Make yourself comfortable." Parker smiles at her and then walks up the stairs to his little room. His leopard is itching to run off some aggression from the little bit of information she's already told him.

Sitting on the bed, he wipes his hands over his face and takes a deep breath, thinking over his conversation with Addison. She doesn't trust easily, well, no shit. She's been through something horrific and she needs to feel safe and protected. And this, somehow, is exactly what he plans on accomplishing.

Parker is all too glad she escaped from 'Mr. I think it's cool to beat on women.' He's hopeful that whatever his real name is, he forgets about her, lets her go, but his gut says the guy will come looking for her. Her abuser won't want her telling anyone what he did to her. Because he'll be going to jail afterward. Parker wants to make sure he's ready for him when he comes looking for Addison and London.

He puts on his shoes and socks then walks out to his truck. He drives about a mile down the road and turns off into a makeshift driveway on his property. He parks the truck about one hundred feet into the woods, gets out, then locks the doors behind him.

Pocketing the keys, he strips off his clothing, putting it all inside the weatherproof compartment in the bed of his truck. Knowing the truck is in the cover of the trees and brush, he walks deeper in the woods, naked.

Parker starts to run and shifts instantly into his leopard, knowing he's deep enough in the trees and there's hardly any vehicles that travel on this road, but safety is first. He wants to make sure he's safe.

Humans don't know of shifters. Only mates know of their true selves. Parker is human, but he has the ability to shift into an animal. He's the only leopard around here. He knows a bear family just in the next town over, good friends of his, and the Sheriff in this area is also a bear shifter. There's also a pack of wolves within fifty miles, but he stays clear of all of them.

Shifters don't have to find another shifter of the same animal to find their mate. Hell, they don't even have to be a shifter to be a mate. A pure human can be a shifter's mate.

As Parker's lithe leopard body runs through the trees and brush, his human self thinks back to the conversation between him and Addison. Remembering back to the money she had in her backpack, too. If she's running with the baby, how invested is this guy in her? Is all that money hers? Does this guy love her at all? Will he come looking for her? Will he try to hurt her? Is she kidnapping London and keeping her from the father? Is the car hers? So many unanswered questions!

As all this is racing around in his brain, his cat growls more and more. Pouncing up and over boulders, around giant pine trees and down a riverbank, splashing through the cool water. It hits him in the face and Parker's human mind slams back.

Does it really matter? Any of that? She's a woman, with a young child and she needs help. His human side says.

She belongs to us. You can see that, can't you? Her smell flows through my nostrils, and I know she's our true mate. Her beauty, her shapely body. She will be ours soon. And we will be whole once again. The cat purrs loudly.

How can she be for us? I've had my soul mate and I killed her. Hailey was severely hurt and lost the baby and I couldn't even get help in time for either of them. Parker shouts at his cat.

She wasn't strong enough to hold on. The Doctor said that the way she fell and the time it took to get to her and back home, she didn't make it. It's not your fault. She was your mate. At the time. She's gone now, and Addison is your other mate. Your true mate. That baby, London, will be your child as well. Hailey was your soul mate, but now you, we, have a second chance. Parker's cat whispers to him in his head.

The leopard's stride falters and he stumbles. Coming to a stop he looks around, realizing they are almost on the edge of the acreage to the south. They've run a good thirty miles. He decides now to turn around and go back, panting the whole way to the truck. Just taking their time to think of a plan to keep Addison and London safe, and what to do with them both.

After shifting, and then getting dressed inside the truck, Parker fires it up and heads back home. He enters the house later in the afternoon, and all is quiet. Walking to the master suite where he finds the door locked. He can only imagine that Addison and London are taking a nap in the master bed, peacefully. Pillows propped around London, so she doesn't fall off.

Parker checks the list Addison made for food and supplies sitting on the kitchen table. He wants to make sure they buy a crib for London to sleep in. Maybe a high chair so she doesn't have to be fed sitting on the floor.

He finds blocks, children's books and a few other kid things strewn across the coffee table in the living room. He walks up to his small bedroom, strips off his clothes and then gets into the shower.

Allowing the heat of the shower spray to calm the ache from his now stretched out muscles and thinking of Addison asleep on the bed, hair mussed and draping over her face a bit, his cock hardens. The woman is downright gorgeous.

Little London looks nothing like her momma so he's guessing she looks like her daddy. Poor girl. But she's beautiful as well. She has a few traits from her mom. Already she has her momma's personality so maybe she will be more like her as she gets older.

Slipping from the heat and steam of the bathroom, he throws on a fresh pair of jeans and a tee, and then walks back down to the main floor. He knocks softly on the door of the bedroom, so he doesn't scare her.

"Addison? Can you unlock the door? I'm home and showered. If you want to come to town with me, we can grab what we need and come right back." He asks through the closed door.

Chapter Three

ADDISON FELT SO tired and she could see London needed a quick nap, too. Parker had already been gone for a few hours, but he did say he had business to take care of in town. She didn't know how far away the town was or what town she was even in. When he came back, hopefully they could get things for London.

She rushes to get the dishwasher going in the kitchen with the dishes they used for breakfast and then she moves into the living room. She glances around, noticing all the toys on the floor from playing with London. She quickly cleans them up and sets them all on the coffee table. This way Parker won't yell at her for leaving toys all over the house. They're technically picked up and won't be stepped on.

With the dishes going and the toys off the floor, he shouldn't have to yell at her or smack her around. He's apologized to her a lot since she's been in his home. She doesn't understand why he's apologizing for things. But what if he's not like that? Yelling, punching, kicking and blaming her for everything? *He's much bigger than Derek. When he hits me, it's going to hurt a lot more. Bruise longer.*

Addison thinks back to Derek's car, and how she ran it off the road. *He's going to kill me for wrecking it, literally, when he finds me, and then he'll kill London because he never wanted her in the first place.*

When Addison left in a hurry early that morning, after Derek had rolled off her from a quick and rough fuck, and he'd fallen asleep, she'd told herself, *no more tears falling because of that demon of a man. I hope he gets run over by karma one day. Maybe get his ass beat by someone, someday.*

She'd had enough of men and them hitting her and putting her down. She has self-worth and is a human being, for Christ sake. *No way am I staying here any longer than I need to. I need to leave and find the car, see how damaged it is so I can keep going. Get to my sister's place.*

Addison's older sister, Vanessa, lives in southern California with her husband, Kenneth and their young daughter, Kiley. She was hoping to get there and stay with her until she could get a job. Support herself and London. Nessa has no idea she left Derek. Addison doesn't even have a cell phone to call and tell her that she was on her way.

While sitting at the table this morning, eating breakfast that Parker had made for her, she couldn't look at him. Derek never wanted her to look him in the eyes unless he was beating her. He wanted to see her tears. Her fear of him made him more powerful.

Addison remembers back when her and Derek first started dating. He used to be a loving man, making good money at his job. Hell, she never even knew what he did for a job. He didn't wear a suit, so it wasn't a fancy office.

She couldn't even say when exactly his personality changed from loving man to a demon monster. It was over time, a gradual change, but not overnight. It was some time after she moved in with him.

Derek would leave by ten in the morning for work and would come home for dinner. He would beat her because there was something wrong with dinner, or the kitchen wasn't clean enough, or whatever other reason he could dream up. There didn't have to be a real one, just something he decided wasn't right and used as an excuse to beat her. Then, thankfully, he would abruptly calm down and would leave again. This had been the routine for weeks, almost every single day for months.

Sometimes he wouldn't come home until well after midnight, reeking of booze and cheap perfume from some other woman. She was sure of it.

Who knows who or what he was doing. He kept a roof over her and London's head and food in the fridge. When she had told him she suspected she was pregnant, he was so pissed. He punched her in the face, then her stomach, then started to kick her in the ribs when she was down.

When he was tired and heavily breathing, he walked out the front door. Later that same evening, he came home with flowers and dessert in to-go boxes.

He had told her he was sorry over and over that night and he made sweet love to her. He was gentle and loving, apologizing profusely and swearing it'd never happen again.

The next night, late in the evening as they'd been watching the football game on television and he'd drunk a couple beers, he'd received a text message then got up and left without saying a word.

Later that night, he came back drunk. He smacked her around again and tore off her clothes, demanding she have sex with him. She didn't want to because she was so sore from the beating and she'd made the mistake of saying *no*. He'd taken his fists to her more, punching her in the kidneys and stomach, kicking her in the ribs and then, finally, when she lied sobbing and bleeding on the floor thinking she could take no more, he grabbed her by the hair and threw her to the bed. It was well after midnight when he sexually assaulted her in their bed.

When he was finally finished fucking her, he pulled out, rolled off her and fell asleep; already snoring before his head hit the pillow. She knew he'd done a number on her this time, and was sure she had cracked ribs, but she managed to crawl to the bathroom and shower.

She wanted so badly to get his vile smell of hard drinking and the stinky, sweet smell of perfume from the other woman off her that she scrubbed her skin raw. All the swirling emotions and smells made her vomit a few times in the shower.

After the water turned cooler, she dried off gently. Already noticing the bruising and welts forming on her face and skin. She pulled a soft white tee shirt over her head and a pair of black shorts up over her hips. Then quietly she climbed back into bed with the demon. She quietly cried herself to sleep, holding her ribs with her arms. She knew that if she was quiet, and made herself small, maybe he'd forget that she was there.

A soft knocking on the bedroom door startles Addison awake, and she freezes in the large king-sized bed, pulling the covers up to her neck, listening, not moving, hardly breathing. A glance over next to her in the bed, reassures her London is still asleep, despite the knocking and the thrashing about she was sure occurred during the nightmare. She must have been dreaming of that monster, remembering that night and all the others just like it. Derek frequented her nightmares often, playing the starring role in her torments almost every night for years, either in her dreams or in reality.

The knocking continued, but then she hears Parker's muffled voice through the closed door, bringing her back to the present in a flash but with a huge sigh of relief. *It's not Derek.*

"Addison? Can you come unlock the door? I'm home and showered. If you want to come to town with me, we can grab what we need and come right back."

She gets up carefully, trying not to disturb the baby. "Oh, sorry," she lamely replies to him in a hushed voice and hurries to unlock the door. She jogs back to the bed and sits with her knees under her chin, wrapping her arms around her legs, pulling herself in tight and small.

Addison remembers sitting like this when Derek would come home, or she would hide under the blankets pretending she was asleep. Not that either one worked, really. If Derek wanted sex, he just took it from her. If he wanted to beat on her, he would.

Seeing the kindness in Parker's eyes, she doesn't think he could ever be evil like Derek. She wants to believe it so bad. It's almost shameful to put both of their names in the same sentence, or in the same thought.

There is no comparison between the two men. Derek is shorter, but only by a few inches at most. He is lean and somewhat muscular, about one hundred eighty pounds and in decent shape.

But the two men, their body structure, way different. Not even close.

Parker is well over two hundred pounds, for sure. Pure, solid muscle, and he's taller by a few inches, she's sure of it. He looks like he'd be a protector of those he loves. But he looks sad. His face lights up when he's around London, but then Addison can see pain behind his eyes too. It makes her curious and she wants to know what puts that look of loss into his gaze.

She watches as Parker walks into the room, cautiously. She knows he's afraid to scare her and she appreciates his consideration. He's always watchful of his movements around her. Not too fast or too close, knowing she doesn't like to be touched. She's had bad touch for too long and doesn't want any kind of touch anytime soon.

Parker slowly sits on the bed, his gaze glancing to the still sleeping London on the other side. He sits back some more, eyes down cast, and folds his hands in his lap. After a pause and a deep breath, he looks back over to London once more and then to Addison.

"She's a pretty little girl you have. How old is she?" He whispers.

"Thank you. She will be a year old in August."

Addison slowly lets go of the death grip she had with her arms around her legs, moving to cross her legs together on the bed. She's learning to relax around Parker and it feels good. She notices him smile at her doing so.

"When will she wake up? I want to get going to town and back because it's quite a drive roundtrip. But I understand the need for her to nap."

He's considerate of her needs. Sweet to know.

"She should wake up soon. I can wake her and change her diaper and we can go now." Addison likes being around Parker. She's starting to feel comfortable and safe around him. Even though it's been a very short time with him. But yet, she can't help but feel guarded. As of now, she gets a good feeling from him, one that tells her he wouldn't hurt her or London, but there's something about him. Something dark lurking there.

"If you could, that would be great. Sorry about cutting her nap short."

She sits forward and puts her hand on his thigh, just above his knee, and he looks her in the eyes, seemingly surprised she's touching him. "It's okay but thank you. It's been a long time since anyone has cared about what her or I need."

She realizes what she's done and jerks her hand back. She used to be a very touchy person. Touching people on the arm when talking, laughing. She misses the positive human contact.

He grabs her wrist, softly, just enough that her gaze flashes to meet his. She knows he can see that the movement he made has startled her, alarmed her.

He lets go immediately, seeing her afraid of him. "I'm sorry, Addison. I didn't mean to startle you. It was just nice that you reached out to me. I've been afraid to touch you."

"I like to be touched." She whispers. "I crave it. But I've been in a…bad relationship for so long. I don't really remember anymore what any other touch feels like other than the negative kind. Hurtful and mean."

Addison is ready to cry at the information she just told Parker. She can feel her eyes pricking with unshed tears and turns away, ducking her head, allowing her long hair to hide her face from him. She's only known this man for less than twenty-four hours and already she's telling him her problems, her deepest secrets.

She knows he could use the information she told him against her. She basically admitted to him that she's been in an abusive relationship. Now, she's afraid of what will happen. Will he call the cops? Turn her in? She's not ready to tell him more about her past, but she needs him to understand that she's fragile. She's going to need time to trust him.

Addison can feel his hand move her hair away from her face and he's leaning forward. She can't stop the flinch when his hand comes into view under her hair. He's only trying to move it out of the way, so he can see her face better.

"Hey, it's okay. You can trust me. I won't hurt you. I've brought you here to my home to help you."

She nods her head, "I know, and I thank you so much. I'm just not ready to tell you everything yet. Okay? Can you respect that, for now?" She wipes away the fallen tears with her other hand and sniffles.

"Yeah, I can. I just hope you can tell me soon, so I know how to expect what's coming." He smiles and swipes his thumb over her tear-streaked cheek.

For once she doesn't flinch at the contact. She closes her eyes and just breathes deep, trying to relax in another man's presence, the soft touch so different.

He's so tender and sweet when his hand touches her cheek, and slowly moves her hair up and over her ear. He's a beautiful man. He has black hair and the prettiest light blue eyes Addison has ever seen. Straight nose and strong jawline. A solid body and muscular chest and shoulders. She noticed that the first day at breakfast. He was wearing a tee shirt and jeans. She could see the bulging of muscles outlined under his shirt then.

Addison couldn't look up at this well-defined man. If Derek ever found out she was here and that she looked at another man in any way, he would beat her senseless. He'd done it before.

Addison had noticed small things already in the home. Like maybe Parker does live here alone. She'd observed a few minor traces of a woman's touch here and there, but nothing clearly saying a woman lives here currently.

Addison still has her eyes closed when suddenly she feels the bed dip and little hands pull on the side of her shirt. London has woken up and Addison wipes her tears quickly away, not wanting her daughter to see her sadness. She beats back the negative emotions, pushing them down into her stomach, and focuses on her one true love, London Sophia. Her reason for existing.

"Hey there, sleepy girl! Should we change you and get ready to go shopping?" Addison sniffs and shows her daughter a brave face, smiling wide.

London giggles and the sound makes Addison's heart feel lighter. She loves her little girl with everything she is.

Derek had learned to tolerate London, and she had learned to tolerate him. She'd figured out fast there was no needing to cry unless there was something wrong.

Derek didn't like her crying, and went after Addison to shut her up, which only made London cry more. Addison figured London had perhaps learned by watching Derek, and that if she stopped crying, he would stop beating Addison.

London never cried anymore, which is a good thing, but Addison wants her to never see that again. She wants her to be happy and laugh. Every child should be able to laugh and cry when needed. Emotions are free. London and Addison; they weren't free. To do anything. Until now.

Chapter Four

ADDISON WANTS TO check on the insurance for the car, hopefully to get it fixed, but she doesn't want them to alert the police. Or Derek. Just in case he reported the car stolen.

Derek has two vehicles, a truck and his car. Addison wasn't allowed to drive either, even though she kept her license valid. She only took his car when she needed it. Milk, bread, whatever, and she always made sure she put gas back in.

Derek would check the mileage occasionally to see what Addison had been doing. If he decided she'd been disobedient, and he randomly did so for any reason, he would beat her. In his mind taking his vehicle to the store to get necessities just wasn't an excuse and he figured she needed to be taught a lesson to make her more compliant.

Addison almost gave in and let him break her, once, but that was before she knew she was for sure pregnant with London. Addison had gotten into the tub, filled it with hot water, and sliced each of her wrists. The sting of the blade biting into her skin had been a good thing at the time. She had wanted it, needed to feel it, to feel anything aside from the way Derek made her feel everyday, like a worthless sack of nothing.

Derek found her soon after she did it and rushed her to the hospital. That's when she found out she was, in fact, pregnant.

They'd gone home later in the week when she'd been released from the hospital under his care, and she told him she was pregnant. Derek had not been happy about her suicide attempt or the pregnancy, and that very night he beat her again, leaving her broken, bleeding, and crying on the floor. He'd told her she belonged to him and he would never let her leave him. If she was going to die, it would be him who would make it happen.

He'd isolated her from everyone and everything, effectively cutting her off from any options, and chance whatsoever of leaving him. She wasn't allowed to have a cell phone, or one even connected in the house. Derek didn't believe they needed one. Addison couldn't leave on her own or sneak away. She'd tried, often, but he would always find her. Those nights the beatings would be worse, and she'd end up in bed healing for days. It'd truly been a wonder she'd never lost the baby.

Mentally shaking away the dark thoughts, Addison glanced down at her wrists, seeing the scars there, a lingering reminder of that day. A reminder of when she'd discovered she wanted to live. She was pregnant. She knew she had love inside of her to give to the unborn baby and it'd had given her the will to go on.

Addison grabs her wallet from her purse, shoving it into the backpack and zipping it closed. She flips the strap over her shoulder, picks up London and slips her over to sit on her hip as they walk out to the living room.

Parker is waiting for her. He smiles, and it warms Addison's hardened heart. She can feel the walls crack. Just a little bit. He truly seems like the perfect man.

Addison nods her head but doesn't smile back. She carries London and the backpack, walking past him and out the front door. He has London's car seat sitting next to the front door already waiting for them. Addison hears him grab it on his way out the door behind her.

She suddenly feels a slight pressure on her lower back, and knows it's his other hand lightly touching her, guiding her out the door. She can feel her body tense up and it's a strange feeling. To be touched and not have it hurt. To be guided through a door. Manners from a man. Maybe this could be a good thing, for a little while anyway.

***

London has been busy playing with her toys in the back seat of the truck, laughing and being a generally happy child despite the long drive into town. She has the cutest giggle. It makes Parker laugh.

Addison even smiles and giggles at her daughter. She, too, has the most beautiful smile, and her laughter, God, it spears Parker straight through his heart. Light, happy and full of life. She's truly happy with her daughter. He can see the absolute love she feels for her child.

Parker had noticed Addison's movements earlier in the bedroom. She'd been hiding her tears, flinching at his touch, then hiding all that emotion when London woke up. She clearly doesn't want her daughter to know when she's sad. He supposed it was Addison's way of protecting London.

He'd noticed the scars on the insides of both of her wrists and they looked old, but still, something, or someone, drove her to do that, gave her a reason to not want to live anymore. He shakes his head at the thought. He couldn't imagine anyone making another person feel like they couldn't exist on this planet anymore.

Parker parks the truck outside of the store, gets out and walks around the other side to open Addison's door.

She looks up at him, startled. "What are you doing?"

"I'm opening your door, helping you out. It's a big step and I don't want you to fall or get hurt." Parker answers her with a big smile on his face. He wonders if no man has ever done this for her before. If so, that's sad.

She gets out of the truck as Parker helps her and she takes his offered hand. The zing is back. He didn't feel it when he guided her out of the house. Must be skin on skin contact.

Addison opens the back door, climbs up and unlatches London from her car seat. Then she grabs the backpack from the floor of the truck and flips it over her shoulder.

Parker notices that when Addison jumps up to get London, her ass is nice and bent over in front of him. He wants to put his hands on her backside and almost does for a hairsbreadth of a second but pulls back just in time.

Addison turns and looks at him, her gaze questioning.

He knows he's been caught looking at her ass and feels a slight heat creep up his neck and over his cheeks. *Shit.* He backs up a bit and he can feel his face warm slightly more.

She frowns and then smiles slightly, like she's realized what he was doing.

"Can you take the back pack, or can you lift her from the seat? I can't do both with your truck so high."

"I can take London, no problem." He helps Addison down from the truck and then reaches for London. The little girl has her arms spread open for him to grab her.

London giggles and snuggles into his neck as Parker pulls her close to his chest. He shuts the door and locks up the truck.

Addison walks next to him as they enter the grocery store and Parker grabs a cart with a child seat and sets London in, then takes the seat belt and straps her in. Addison puts the backpack in the main area of the cart.

Addison pushes the cart and Parker grabs what they need for supplies from the list in his hand and adds them to the cart.

Addison grabs a few other items for London as well. By the time they're finished getting food and extra items for the little drool bucket, Parker is in shock at how full the cart is. As they walk up to the cashier, Parker admits to Addison, "I never knew kids would need so much stuff."

Addison nods her head. "She only needs a few things, food wise she's pretty easy now that she can start to eat real food. Diapers and wipes are a necessity, though." She smiles slightly.

Setting the items on the conveyer, Parker notices Addison unstrap London and she grabs the backpack. When Parker turns to speak to her, she looks terrified. Absolutely scared out of her mind. Her face has gone pale and she looks like she's about to cry or throw up.

"Addison, what's wrong?" Parker whispers in her ear and he tries to wrap his arm around her waist. Parker's leopard is pacing, sensing Addison's discomfort and is on high alert.

"I have to hide…I mean…use the restroom…check London's diaper." Her voice is trembling and her eyes lock on a man walking on the sidewalk out front of the store.

She knows him. This is the man who she's running from. "Go Addison, go take London to the restroom. I'll take care of things here." Parker tips her chin so she gazes into his eyes and she nods her head, understanding what he's said and knowing he's got this. She walks swiftly to the back of the store with London.

"Bingo asshole, I've got you now." Parker whispers under his breath. He sees the asshole that's been terrorizing her and commits his face to memory. Sight. Sound of his gait. The scent of him as he walks into the store and looks around casually. Parker's leopard is growling and hissing in his head. *I want to kill this man for everything he put our mate through.*

Parker keeps an eye on the asshole while the clerk rings their items and bags them up. This man is looking for Addison. Parker knows she won't leave her hiding place until he goes and gets her. Parker calms down enough to pay for everything and loads up his truck.

The man leaves the store after a few more minutes, as Parker is finishing putting the roll cover back on the bed of the truck; then locking it down. Parker returns to the store and finds his way back to the restrooms. His cat is worried for their two ladies.

Parker knocks on the door quietly, opening it slightly and peeking inside, "Addison, are you in here, honey? He's gone. He left." He says quietly. He knows she's terrified. Her whole body was physically shaking when she saw the man.

Parker sees the far bathroom stall open and Addison peeks out. She's been crying.

Screw it. Parker walks into the bathroom and pulls her out of the stall and right into his arms, while she's holding London. He grabs London from her arms and Addison wraps both arms around Parker's waist.

She bursts into tears, her head resting against Parker's chest and he pulls her closer, feeling her trembling against him. London pets her momma's hair. Watching daughter soothing her mother pulls at Parkers heart in a way he never imagined he could feel. This little girl, trying to comfort her mommy as only an eight-month-old can. Parker pulls her closer still as she lets out her tears onto his tee shirt.

Fifteen minutes later, Parker's finally convinced Addison that Derek has left the store. She finally gives in, so they can drive to the baby store to get London a crib. She had argued a bit at first because she doesn't have a way to travel with it when she leaves, but she eventually gives in.

Parker tries to hide the hurt and sting from her words about leaving. But he's not sure if she saw it or not. He doesn't want Addison or London leaving, running away. He wants them to stay with him where he's keeping them safe.

If she leaves, Derek could find her. There's nothing that Parker can do about holding her to him, unless he ties her to the bed, but that's a totally different dream. Unless he can prove to Addison that she's his true mate. He's content with her around and is unhappy about her saying she's going to leave. Even the leopard inside of Parker is nervous at her decision to leave.

Parker parks the truck in front of the baby store a few minutes later, and he helps Addison with London once again.

***

An hour later, Parker finds himself shoving a crib box and a new high chair in the bed of the truck then locking it up tight. He also bought London a few outfits he thought were cute.

On their way home, Addison is quietly sitting next to Parker. He's paid for everything today. The food. The crib. Saved her from the bathroom and comforted her. He was happy that she was at least in his arms, even though she was upset. His inner cat was purring when she was there. He doesn't think it was loud enough for her to hear, and if she did, she didn't say anything about it.

She came willingly and wrapped her arms around him without trouble or being afraid of him. He hopes maybe she's starting to trust him, finally.

Parker wants to hold her in his arms again, and soon. He feels content. Happy. Whole with her in his arms. It's a strange feeling, because when he had Hailey in his arms, it wasn't like this. Close, but this is…more. This is so much more.

Parker loved Hailey and they were married for a year before she became pregnant. He loved her with everything he had, and they were happy living here in this big home. The night she died…he no longer slept in the master bedroom.

He's been in the small room upstairs since then, not being able to sleep in the big bedroom without her there. Now that Addison is here, it isn't strange being in there. It feels…right. And he's confused by that thought.

Parker can go in the master bedroom now and have it not be uncomfortable. It's like it's okay now. Someone else is in there; she belongs in there. It's a feeling like Parker can be in there with Addison and there's no conflict, no tension in the air surrounding him anymore.

If a shifter is mated to another and that mate dies, is there another mate for the shifter left behind? Do I have another soul mate out there? Is there more than one shifter mate for everyone? Parker mulls over those questions with his leopard.

The inner leopard tells Parker, *I remember, a long time ago, hearing your parents talking about there can be three in a shifter circle, a triad. But don't remember anything about getting a second chance at love with another soulmate. But why wouldn't there be?*

Do you think Addison could be our second chance at love? Could Addison be our soul mate even if she's human? Parker asks his leopard.

I'm not sure, but this feels right. The leopard purrs back, snuggling in to that thought.

During this inner turmoil inside Parker's head, their own private conversation, he turns to glance over at Addison and London, seeing they have fallen asleep. Content and sated, hopefully feeling safe for the first time in a long time. Both his ladies.

Earlier, they had stopped for dinner before heading home, knowing it would be way after dark by the time they arrived. He's thankful for the self-sustaining coolers in the bed of his truck to keep the food cold.

Parker drives down the long driveway to his home, over a mile of essentially a dirt road winding around the huge pines surrounding his land. Up and over Sandy creek, and the river isn't that far away either.

Pulling up to the house, Parker puts his truck in park and turns off the ignition. It's after ten-thirty and he's tired. He glances over at her and notices the soft glow from the dashboard lights gives Addison an angelic glow to her face. She's so stunningly beautiful.

Parker shakes Addison's shoulder softly, waking her up carefully, so she doesn't startle. She slowly opens her eyes, focusing on Parker, realizing where she's at. "Are we home already?" She mutters.

He likes how she already considers it as her 'home' without even thinking of it. She's becoming more comfortable around him, clearly, and he's very happy about that. His leopard purrs in agreement.

"Yeah, we're home. Do you want me to carry London into the house or can you do it by yourself?" Parker askes her, knowing she's still tired.

"No, I've got her. Thanks, though. Are you able to get everything into the house by yourself? I'll come back out after I get her to bed and help you put everything away." She whispers.

He chuckles quietly. "You get her inside and tucked into bed. I can get everything else. Yes, if you don't mind, you can come out to help me when you're done." He whispers back.

Parker reaches back to unbuckle London from her baby carrier, so Addison can grab her sleeping body quietly.

Parker gets out of his side of the truck, rounds the front end and opens Addison's door, helping her down. He picks up the sleeping child carefully and puts her into Addison's waiting arms.

Addison grabs the backpack, too, and then walks into the house, flicking on the front light.

Parker unlocks the bed of the truck and starts to bring the bags of food into the kitchen, setting them on the counters. He grabs the crib box next and sets it in the living room. He decides that will be his first job tomorrow. Then he goes back for the high chair and a few extra bags.

Addison walks out from the master bedroom about fifteen minutes later, shutting the door behind her. She makes her way into the kitchen, she notices that Parker has brought everything in from the truck and the counters and floor are full of bags, she flinches but doesn't say a word.

She helps Parker put away all the food and other items they bought. They don't get in each other's way; at all, oddly. It's like they move in sync with one another, almost a dance around the kitchen where neither partner touches.

Just like Hailey and I used to do, but better.

After everything is in place, Parker grabs a beer from the fridge, popping the top off and taking a long drink of the cold brew. He offers

Addison one, but she shakes her head and an odd look crosses her face.

He walks over and plops his tired ass on the couch, blowing out a long, exhausted breath. Setting the beer on the side table, he sprawls out across the couch, stretching his long legs out and his feet up on top of the coffee table. He pushes over the toys left there with his foot. Parker tips his head back against the cushion of the couch. He then spreads out his arms, resting them across the back of the couch.

***

Addison watches Parker and takes it all in. Him grabbing the beer, drinking it and watching his neck muscles swallow the alcohol. She almost stares as he sets the bottle on the end table and then fully relaxes back into the couch.

He's an amazingly handsome man. Relaxed in his home. He can be himself here. He doesn't have to watch what he does. No one here to tell him what to do. What to say, how to act. Just to do what he wants to when he wants to do it. *Must be nice to be able to live like this.*

She's hesitant on what to do. She could tell him good night, it is late, but then she did sleep in the truck on the way back. She could sit next to him and tell him a little bit about herself. He said he wanted to know more about her, after all.

She's feeling much more comfortable with him, and that scares her. She shouldn't be comfortable with anyone. That's how mistakes are made. That's how Derek happened.

She feels comfortable and safe here with Parker. *Home.* Yes, this feels like home. Or what a home should feel like. *Home. Yeah. That sounds nice. Too bad I have to move on from here. I don't want Derek to find out I'm shacking up with another man. He'd kill Parker. too.*

Addison flicks her gaze back to Parker, then around the room, conflicted on what to do. She takes a step closer to him, again looking around the room, her fingers in front of her, slowly fidgeting and clasping her sweaty palms. She is nervous, no doubt about that, but she's determined to push it aside in the hope he won't notice. She gets to the coffee table and pushes the toys to the far end of the coffee table, so Parker won't kick them and knock them to the floor.

"Is it okay that I sit here with you? I don't mean to make you uncomfortable. I can go to my room for the night." She asks timidly while leaning away from him, perched on the very edge of the couch, eyes downcast.

***

Parker can feel her gaze on him, judging his reaction, but doesn't move to look, he already knows Addison is thinking about something, but she doesn't know what to do about it. A minute later, he feels the couch dip next to him and Addison's scent lingers in his nose.

Parker can feel her move closer, then she slides into his side, under his arm, resting her head on his chest. He lifts his head and looks at the top of her head. Addison glances up and pulls away from him and he can feel the cooler air take over where her body's warmth was.

"No, it's okay. You can come to me for anything, Addison. To talk to me. A shoulder to cry on. A hug or even a place to rest your head, even if it's only for a few minutes." He answers her truthfully.

Addison looks in to Parker's eyes, searching for the truth in what he's just said. She must have found it because she lays her head back on his chest, her hand curled under her chin, and she brings her knees up to her chest. Snuggling into his warmth.

Parker's fighting against himself. He wants to lower his arm and bring her closer, to make her feel safe, protected. He makes his decision, finally, and then moves slowly.

She turns her head to look. After she sees his arm, she snuggles back in and lays her hand on his chest. She huffs out a breath and he knows now he has her trust.

She's huddled in a ball against his side. Her hands folded under her chin. Her feet under her ass and she's leaning into him. She's warm and content and trusting him to protect her.

After an hour or so of having Addison snuggling into his side, Parker can tell by her even breathing that she's fallen asleep. She's still huddled into him and he shifts to lift her up and against his chest. He walks her to the bedroom carefully, laying her down and covering her up.

London is snuggled on the other side of the bed and is covered under the extra blanket he gave her the first night.

After leaving them safely in the room, he shuts the door and grabs his now warm beer from the end table. Dumping the remaining beer down the kitchen sink and throwing the bottle away, he turns off the lights and locks the front door.

Parker slowly walks upstairs to his own room, thinking of Addison the whole way. Now that he knows that this guy is here looking for her, he's not taking any chances with Addison and London's safety.

Parker strips off his clothes and climbs into bed naked. It's too late for a shower or a run. So, he grabs the light sheet and pulls it up to his chest.

Sleep comes fast, and he dreams about the beautiful young woman downstairs who's slowly stealing his heart.

Chapter Five

ADDISON WAKES UP to use the bathroom and notices she's in her bed and not on the couch with Parker. To her surprise, she's disappointed to be here in the bed. She glances at the clock on the night table. 6:36 a.m.

She's recently found there's a bathroom connected to this bedroom that is quite luxurious. A huge garden tub with jets. A full shower with two shower heads coming from the ceiling.

She hasn't investigated it too much yet, but she plans on going to shower there soon. Hell, why not now? It's still early, and she knows London won't be waking up anytime soon. At least for another hour or two. It's been two days since she's showered, and she really does need one.

Convinced it's the best time, she jogs over to her suitcase and pulls out her shower things. She walks into the bathroom.

The night Addison fled with London, she'd showered at the hotel. She got a phone call from the front desk clerk mentioning that there was a man asking about her. She'd thought he looked like trouble, so she called to warn her.

Addison had immediately starting packing everything up quickly. Her and London left as soon as she had everything packed up and she creeped out to the parking lot and took off. Thank God she'd parked around the back, and he didn't get to see the car.

Addison had sped off into the night around two in the morning. A few miles down the road is when she'd seen the deer in the middle of the road. She'd veered to the side to avoid hitting the damn thing and that's how she'd ended up in the ditch and smashed up Derek's car.

She was going to have to go back there and try to get the car out, and make sure she has everything she needs out of there. She has the backpack, purse, box of diapers, and suitcase. She thinks that's all she had with her.

She stands in the shower now, soaking up all the heat into her muscles. Letting the hot water wash away the stress and grime of the past few days.

As she's washing her hair and body, she also shaves her legs. She hasn't done that in a few days, and it feels good. To take time for herself because she wants to, not because she has to for someone else. Derek wanted her shaved. Legs, armpits, and lady parts.

She hates shaving the lady parts. Trim, yes, but not shaved.

After about a half an hour in the heated warmth of the shower, she steps out onto the fluffy mat on the floor. Grabbing the towel from the towel bar, she wraps it around her body, tucking it in between her breasts to secure it there. She grabs another towel and starts drying her hair with it.

She then starts tackling the tangled locks with her brush, brushing out the long, straight strands until all the knots are gone and it's shiny, flowing almost to her rear end now.

Unwrapping the towel from her body, she begins drying her body. Lovely, soft and fluffy towels, not the coarse cheap one's she's used to. These are heavenly.

After hanging up the towels and then putting on clean clothes for the day, she realizes she only grabbed a few sets of clothing from the house. At the time, London was more important, and she'd grabbed everything she thought London could still wear.

Addison does have one passion, though, and she's going to keep doing it, if she can afford it. Nice panties and bra sets. She loves them! They make her feel sexy and empowering. She only has a few sets left because Derek would rip them from her when he wanted sex. He loved them, too. *Asshole.*

She double checks the bathroom, making sure everything is put away where she found it. She cleans up her shower things and puts them back in her suitcase. She never knows when she might have to up and leave again quickly. She learned early with that one. Always be prepared.

Derek would attack or have violent sex with Addison then pass out. She remembers that she would cry in her pillow after he would fall asleep. When he was doing those things to her, she would show no emotion and just lay there. He'd beat her for that, too. Because she wasn't showing any emotion. *Like I'm supposed to enjoy that shit, I don't think so.*

Maybe I could like a little rough sex, when I know a man can take charge and show his dominate side, but not cross the line like Derek always did. I'm sure I could learn to enjoy sex. But not by him anymore. I would rather die before Derek takes me to hell again. Never again. Addison hopes karma comes and runs him over and shoves a stick up his ass so far, he'll look like a stuffed pig about to be put on a barbeque!

Addison realizes she's getting angry and she needs to relax. London's starting to stir and she's being too loud with her huffing and puffing. She crawls back into bed and snuggles London next her. The baby calms Addison and centers her. She's Addison's little Zen.

Lying next to London, she thinks back to yesterday and the things they did with Parker in town. Seeing Derek walking into the store nearly undid her. She couldn't escape fast enough. She couldn't run fast enough with London but didn't want to attract attention for him to notice her.

She hid in the bathroom crying into London's little shirt. Trying to keep her quiet as well. Parker said he would take care of it and he did.

Parker had walked right into the women's restroom and she remembers how she immediately flew into his arms of protection. She and London really are protected by Parker. Safe.

Addison knows that Parker will never hurt them. He's a protector of some kind. Even with the little bit of darkness she can see in his eyes, he's all good. She feels like she can trust him with London's life. With *her* life.

Suddenly, Addison hears knocking on the bedroom door, pulling her from her drowsy nap. It's light out now, maybe after nine, and she knows it's Parker at the door. "Come in," she tells him quietly.

London stirs next to Addison and her beautiful blue eyes open to see her. Addison rubs her rounded tummy and London's legs come up, bringing the blanket with her, tangled around her feet. She grabs her own toes and giggles.

Parker opens the door and smiles at the two of them.

Addison's still under the blankets and quickly sits up, leaning against the headboard. She pushes the blankets down and off her body quickly. She'd learned from that mistake, too.

Derek had come in to the bedroom one time and jumped on Addison while she was sleeping in bed, covered head to toe with the blanket. She'd thought that if she was under the blankets, he couldn't hurt her. Boy, was she wrong. He'd straddled her lap and punched and slapped her. She couldn't move. She'd been trapped under the blankets.

Addison can feel her breathing increase. She slams her eyes shut, holding her closed fists to her eyes, trying to push the visions and thoughts of him and those days away. She can see Derek and she's trying to push him from her mind. She's trapped in a memory.

It's Parker. Not Derek. It's Parker. It's Parker.

"Yes, honey, it's Parker. I'm here. It's me. No one else, just me."

Addison can hear him, so she assumes she must have spoken out loud. She opens her eyes suddenly and sees Parker sitting on the bed next to her, looking concerned. Her breathing is still heavy and labored, panicking.

He's close to her and she lunges out and wraps her arms around his neck, crying into his light blue tee shirt. She can feel his arms circle her waist and he holds her tightly to him.

His body is hard and muscular. Her curvy body fills in the grooves and contours around him. They fit together perfectly. As her breathing evens out, her crying slowly stops, Addison ducks her head down and uses her shirt to hide her face, wiping her nose and tears on the inside of her tee shirt.

She eventually sits back and finishes wiping away her tears. London sits up on the bed, looking at her momma like she's going to cry, too but holds back the tears, just in case. London looks to Parker and then back to Addison. She decides that Parker is a good man and she allows her tears to finally fall. Addison picks her up and holds her close. Snuggling her to her chest. Comforting her small body.

"I'm so sorry, baby. So, sorry. Mommy's just having a bad moment. Give me time." Addison whispers into London's ear.

"Addison, you're allowed to have bad moments. Hell, have a bad month or two. You're scared of what that man did to you and you have every right to feel that way. I hope you can tell me someday soon all about it, so I can help you heal. It's okay, Addy, I'm here." Parker tells her, looking like he means every single word he says. Addison believes him.

He scoots closer to Addison on the bed and she allows him to wrap his arm around her shoulders, comforting her. He uses his other hand to rub London's back up and down, soothing her, too.

Addison settles in next to Parker, resting her head on his chest, and she slowly tells him about where and whom they are running from. She feels Parker tense when she tells him Derek liked to hit and punch whenever he felt it was needed, which was pretty much all the time.

Over the next hour, Addison tells Parker everything, and everything is laid out in front of him like ugly, infected stab wounds to her and London both. Addison pouring out what their lives had been like living with that monster.

Parker sits next to her listening and saying only a few words, questioning some things he needs clarified. Holding Addison's hand in his, his thumb caressing the scars on her wrists.

Addison tells him about that dark point in her life, too. She shudders at the memory and he hugs her closer, mentally giving her his strength and support. He's been listening to everything Addison's told him, letting her get it all out in the hope it'll help her heal. Everything. Every dark thing that demon has done to her.

When she's done telling her story, Parker finally tells her about what happened at the store. "Addison, he was looking for you both. I watched him go up every row and every aisle, searching for you. Then he left and walked down the street after he couldn't find you. I was loading everything into the truck while he was looking around the store. I locked up the truck and came back to get you when I saw him leave the store. He drove off in a black pick-up truck." He sucks in a deep breath and then continues. "I know he won't give up looking for you. I will get rid of him. He won't ever bother you again and you won't live in fear of him anymore, I promise you that."

Addison nods and her voice is trembling from crying, "Yeah, that's his truck. I took his car. I have to go check on it soon and make sure I got everything from it."

"No need. I checked all over that car, I took whatever I found. Let's get London something to eat." Parker attempts to change the topic, knowing Addison is drained and they've both dealt with enough emotional upheaval today.

Parker stands up from the bed, grasping Addison's hand and pulling her up with him. He wraps his arms around her shoulders, pulling her tight to his chest. Wrapping her arms around his back, she inhales his scent and he can feel her calming, the tension fading from her body.

London whines, reminding them she hasn't had her bottle, and Addison pulls away from him. She picks up the child and shifts London to her hip, carrying her out to the kitchen and setting her on the floor. Grabbing a clean bottle from the counter, she pours some milk into the bottle and hands it to the little girl.

"We should probably eat as well." Parker pushes away from the doorjamb where he'd been watching Addison tend to the child.

He walks over to the fridge and pulls things out for breakfast. Eggs, milk, and a loaf of bread. He pulls out a pan and begins to crack eggs into a bowl.

***

Addison sits at the kitchen table and watches him move around the kitchen. As he whisks the eggs, then dips the bread slices one by one into the mixture then sets them to the hot pan, she watches his face and she can tell he's still thinking about what she told him. There's a lot to mull over and she knows he's pissed at what Derek has done to her and London. Who wouldn't be?

Parker sets down a steaming plate of food in front of her. "Thank you, it looks wonderful." She tells him in a quiet voice.

London crawls over to Addison, pulling herself up using the chair leg and her jeans. She feeds London small squishy bites from her fork and she watches her gobble them down.

After they finish their food and clean up, Parker asks Addison, "Can you help me put the crib together?"

"Sure. It shouldn't take too long." She responds.

With assistance from London, and her banging parts together, they have the crib together in under an hour.

It's stunning and beautiful. The warm brown from the oak color makes it look inviting to sleep in. Addison puts sheets and a blanket over the mattress, and then throws in a few plush toys. They push it into the corner of the master bedroom and when that's all done, it's almost time for London's nap.

No more sleeping in bed with Addison or in her car seat. Now, she has her own bed. Her own blankets. And Addison doesn't have to worry about her rolling out of bed or lying too close to her.

***

Parker goes out later that night after the girls are asleep. His leopard is feeling cooped up and needs a good stretch. It's been a few days since he's allowed his inner cat to take over and the animal has been pacing back and forth inside his head, clawing to get out and run.

He heads to where Addison ditched the car, and as he's coming up over the ridge of the embankment he realizes the car's gone. That asshat's scent is everywhere around this place, though. He must have found it and pulled it out.

Thank God for the rain that came and washed most of his horrid scent away earlier in the evening, but now Parker can't tell how long it's been since the evil man has been here. It could have been last week or last night. The spring rains have washed almost all his scent away.

Dammit!

Chapter Six

A FEW WEEKS have gone by since Parker first rescued Addison and London. *I haven't seen or scented Derek in or around town since I went to go check on Addison's car, so maybe he's moved on.*

Don't count on it. Maybe he's searching another town. But I have a feeling he'll be back. His leopard whispers in his head.

Yeah, that's what I'm afraid of.

Parker's inner cat is constantly in a state of agitation lately, pacing within Parker's head. Contemplating over what he wants to do when Derek finally comes slithering back to try to grab Addison. Images flash in his brain, and they are not particularly nice images to have every day.

Parker can't get that demon out of his head. *His face. He's evil. He wants her. He wants her back. He won't get her. He won't touch her. He won't look at her. She's mine. She's always been mine.*

Parker can feel the rip of the leopard taking over. He tears through his clothes and transforms from human to leopard right there on the front porch just from the agitation. Snarling and growling, he takes off running into the woods.

He can feel the pull of his cat's claws into the damp earth as he runs through the woods. Splashing through the river and over boulders that are in his path, feeling the water trickle through his fur, the sharp rocks beneath his pads, the softness of the forest floor compressing under his weight and strength.

The muscle and sinew pulling and stretching as his body pushes them further and deeper into the forest. A rabbit changes its course as Parker runs by it. His cat is not even interested the chase at this point and time. He just wants to run out his anger. Frustration. Planning his revenge for Addison against Derek.

He wonders if Derek has come back to town a few times looking around the stores and restaurants. Derek knows she's here. It will only be a matter of time before they're all in the same spot at the same time. There have been times where Parker can smell a hint of the man's scent here and there. Almost like he's been walking in town, but it's faded away.

He wants to kill the man for what he's done to Addison and for what a bastard he's been as a father to London. He'd better not stop and talk to Addison on the street somewhere when Parker's around, because when he's done with him, the asshole will be praying for Parker to send him back to the hell he came from.

Parker's leopard slows and then stops next to a large pine tree, panting. He stretches his large front legs and paws, then extends his thick claws against the tree, slowly scraping down the bark. He drops down on all fours and then stretches out each hind leg and his back. He lets out a yawn and shakes out his fur.

He trots down to the river's edge, drinking in some of the cool running water and enjoys the coolness on his tongue as it slides down his throat. When he's had his fill, he lifts his head to sniff the air around him, checking out his surroundings. Feeling better after his leopard has made his rounds and lashed out his aggression, resulting in at least some stress lifted off his shoulders, he starts heading back home at a trot.

Parker can smell a rabbit nearby. He sniffs it out as he gets closer to it, and the rabbit startles and takes off running. The leopard takes off after it in a quick chase, resulting in a fast catch and meal. *That was too easy. Almost boring.* His hunger somewhat sated, he trots back home at a comfortable pace.

Still in leopard form, he breaks through the opening of the woods and sees the house, noticing a figure on the front porch rocking in the chair. *It's Addison. Shit.* He fades backward into the blackness of the night, thankful for the cover of the bushes and trees surrounding him. Addison doesn't know Parker's a shifter yet and it's not like he can just walk around. Oregon doesn't have leopards just roaming around the woods.

It's still very early morning and Parker's wondering why Addison is up at this hour. She doesn't have London with her and the door is open with the screen shut.

She's sipping from a mug, so he's guessing coffee, but why now? At this early hour? What's made her so upset she would seek out the darkness for comfort?

He waits her out, sitting back on his haunches under the cover of the trees, watching her. A few minutes later, Addison gets up and goes into the house again, shutting the door behind her.

Parker lies down in the tall grasses and rolls over on his back rubbing it into the ground. The leopard jumps up and shakes out the grass, leaves and whatever else he's picked up rolling around. He slowly creeps up to the house, watching and listening for any noises inside. Nothing. Everything is quiet. He's assuming she went back to bed.

He quickly shifts back to his human form as he walks around to the back door. It's closest to the laundry room and he can slip on a pair of shorts or something.

Parker opens the back door and shuts it behind him with a quiet snick when he enters the small room, naked. Quickly finding a pair of jeans from the other day, he slides both legs in, and zips up the zipper but doesn't do the button.

He walks out into the kitchen, then through the living room. Addison must be in her room. *Whew.* He wouldn't begin to know how to explain walking in the house naked to her. It will be a while before he knows if she'll be able to handle that kind of news.

Oh, by the way, yeah, I can change my form into a very large, black leopard, but it's okay. I won't hurt you. That may just send her screaming. Parker chuckles at the thought, shaking his head.

He makes his way up to his room and pulls off his jeans, tossing them on the floor. He takes a quick shower to wash off the woods, and then climbs into bed, hoping sleep claims him quickly.

Parker knows Addison's a quiet person. A very private, quiet, and innocent in a way. But what she's been through, she's beaten down and he wants to protect her, shelter her from everyone. But doing that won't make her independent. He wants to build her back up.

She needs to find her voice. Parker knows it's there. He's heard it when she talks about London. She's a momma bear with claws out protecting her cub. She's stronger than she thinks. She's shown him already in the past few weeks, and she's becoming stronger by the day.

He's only heard what happened to her, but he wants to know her pain, what she suffered. He wants to pull that pain from her, so she doesn't have to weigh the burden of it anymore.

Parker doesn't only shift into an animal, he heals very quickly. All shifters have fast healing and slow aging. He's also able to share his thoughts and conversations with his mate, parents and siblings telepathically. He can increase or decrease the level of emotion someone feels. This is only for some shifters, not all. And not all leopards have these powers.

When a shifter mates with a human, the shifter powers of fast healing and slow aging goes to their mate. Any children (or cubs) conceived will manifest those powers of shifting, healing, slow aging and any other powers mother nature decides to give them.

If two of the same kind of shifters mate, that will make that blood line thicker. If two different shifters mate, the baby produced will be all one or the other. No half bear and half leopard, or any other mix of two different kinds of shifters can exist.

Chapter Seven

ADDISON JUST COULDN'T sleep last night. She kept feeling afraid, like something is on its way. Something big. And she's uneasy. She went to go sit on one of the rocking chairs on the front porch with a mug of hot chocolate. She wanted to listen to the crickets and night sounds and let them calm her, but moments into her nighttime reprieve, she felt like she was being watched so she went back inside, put her mug in the sink and went back to the safety of her bed.

She woke up tired, her insides all in knots. The sun is up, and she turns to check on London. She's not in her crib or in bed with her.

Addison sits straight up in bed, panicking. "London? Honey, where are you?"

Suddenly, Addison hears a squeal from the other side of the bedroom door and she races over to it, opening it frantically. She sees London and Parker sitting on the floor together building block towers and knocking them down. She runs over to her and picks her up, cradling her to her chest.

She lets her baby's smell soothe her, calming her before she pulls the child's face from her shoulder, her breathing finally calming. She hears Parker get up from the floor and she leans into him as he wraps both of them in his arms.

"Addison, I didn't mean to frighten you. I heard her and didn't want you to wake up. You needed your sleep."

Addison nods her head and takes another deep breath.

A few minutes go by and she finally releases her hold on London and sets her back down on the floor. She sits on the couch and holds her hands over her face, hiding her tears.

Parker sits down with her and slowly rubs his palm over her back.

She huffs out a breath and sits up, dropping her hands to her lap, her face damp from the tears she wiped away. "I'm sorry, Parker. I woke up and she wasn't there, and I panicked. I didn't know where she was."

"It's okay. I'm sorry. I changed her diaper and fed her some small pieces of toast and her milk. Hope that was okay?" He looks like he lost his puppy.

"Yes, thank you for doing that. I was tired and didn't sleep well last night. I came out onto the porch with a cup of cocoa and listened to the night animals. It was soothing and then I went back to bed. Hope I didn't wake you."

"No, you didn't wake me. I was up already. I went for a walk in the woods when you and London were asleep. That calms me." He chuckles a bit.

"Oh, okay. I tried to be quiet anyway." Addison huffs out another breath and stands up, heading in the direction of her room, calling over her shoulder. "I'm going to take a shower, is that okay? You okay with watching her for a bit longer?"

It's not like she hasn't taken a shower with London in the bathroom with her before. And if he doesn't want to watch her, Addison will take her in with her.

"Addison, I've got her. What's wrong?" He asks, walking over to her, concern etching his face.

"I just had a small panic attack when I didn't see her in bed with me or the crib. I'm afraid. I'm terrified Derek will find us." Addison can feel a tear slip over her cheek.

Parker walks to her and wipes the moisture away with his thumb. He pulls her into his chest, wrapping his strong arms around her shoulders.

She breathes in his scent, slowly. He always smells so good. Clean. Musky and all male.

Addison feels him kiss her forehead and then he rests his chin on the top of her head. He breathes in deep, then snuggles his face into her shoulder.

"Addison. He won't do anything to you or London as long as I'm still breathing. You're safe with me." He whispers into her hair and shoulder.

Addison nods her head and pulls from him, already missing the safety she feels in his arms.

But she's not here to be with Parker. She's not looking for another man. She's on the run, and she should call her sister to let her know where she is. Let her know she's safe.

"I'm going to take a shower now. Can I use your phone to call my sister when I get out? I want to let her know I'm safe."

"Yes, you can use my cell."

Addison nods again and makes her way to the bedroom. She turns around once she's in the room and looks back to meet Parker's gaze as she shuts the door.

She lets out her breath in a huff, not realizing that she was holding it. She brushes her hair away from her face with her fingers and then pulls out some clean clothes from her suitcase.

Walking into the bathroom, she sets the clothes on the corner of the sink and turns on the water in the shower, adjusting the temperature.

Stripping out of her clothes, and letting them fall to the tiled floor, she steps into the warm flowing water, letting it wash away the fear and unease of earlier.

After a thirty-minute shower, she dries herself and gets dressed in a pair of soft washed jeans, a pink v-neck tee shirt, and white socks, and then starts to blow dry her hair.

Addison doesn't want it to get comfortable with Parker watching London. She's Addison's child, her responsibility. She puts her things away quickly and rushes out of her room, intent on taking care of her child.

Halfway down the hall, Addison can hear London squealing again. She jogs to the living room and she sees Parker standing and holding London above his head. He clasps her around the ribs, his hands under her arms, and then brings her back down to his face, where he blows raspberry kisses on her belly. The child squeals again in excitement and laughter.

Addison relaxes instantly. The sight of Parker taking such good care of her daughter, almost a loving, tender, parental care, is reassuring even if it's entirely new to her.

Parker is taking such good care of her daughter. Addison can relax and breathe easier knowing her child is safe, cared for, loved.

"I'm sorry it took me so long. I can take her now and you can do whatever we were keeping you from."

"Addison, she isn't a bother to me. You're not a bother to me, either. It's nice to have voices and laughter in this house again. It's okay that you need to take time for yourself. It's fine. I'm happy that I can watch her for an hour or more for you. She's easy to take care of." He tickles the child's belly once more, bringing another round of squealing laughter from London.

"I just don't want you to feel like you have to take care of her when she's my responsibility." Addison whispers, her eyes cast to the floor and her fingers twisting together.

"Addison, come here." He sets London down on the floor by her toys and he holds out his hand for Addison to take. "I can watch her anytime you need. I understand the need for a shower or to prepare food without someone hanging on you."

Addison walks over to him and he inches his hand into hers. She's still nervous but not shaking in terror anymore. He's gentle, caring and meticulously cautious when he's around her. Knowing what happened to her and her past, he's very cautious; and she admires him for it.

"Addison. You know I won't hurt you. Can I hold you for a bit and ease your concern? I want you to trust me, but I know it will take time." He whispers, "Let me in, Addison. Just let me in and I'll show you that I'm not even close to that demon."

Letting Parker pull her to him, she rests her cheek on his chest and listens to his steady beat of his heart. He holds her tightly to him but it's not smothering, not frightening at all. This is a big moment for her. This is Addison trusting Parker, completely. She hasn't let Parker hold her or snuggled into him since that one night when she fell asleep against his chest on the couch.

Parker wraps one of his muscular arms and hand around her shoulders and the other one brushes down her hair, holding her close to him.

She snuggles into his chest. *Safe. Protected.* She knows, now, one hundred percent that he will never hurt her or London. Ever. Parker is her protector. Let that demon come for her. She feels confident and secure that he won't harm her because she has Parker here protecting them.

She can feel tears building up behind her eyelids and she squishes her eyes tightly together, not wanting him to see her vulnerability.

Addison presses her face into his chest and breathes deeply. God, he smells so good. He smells like the pine trees, earthy, and like home. She pulls his scent deeper into her senses, imprinting it within her heart, her mind, her entire essence so she never forgets what he smells like. She feels him rest his chin on top of her head.

He feels like a safe home. Wait. He's not my home. Hell, he's not even mine. Wait. What the hell am I thinking? I'm on the run. I'm hiding out from a demon who will come try to kill me and my daughter, and I'm thinking I have a new man in my life.

She pushes away from Parker and she can see the hurt and confusion in his face, just for a second. "I'm sorry, Parker. I can't be close to you. I feel protected and safe here, with you. And I know you would never hurt London, or me, but I can't get close to you. I don't need a man to make me complete anymore. I had that, and he tore me down. Ripped me apart in every way imaginable and I won't allow it to happen again. We can be friends. Only friends. Okay?"

Her chin quivers and she can feel those traitorous tears start to fall. Even saying the words tears her apart. She looks up into his eyes and she can feel her tears fall, but she pleads for him to understand.

Parker backs up, giving her the distance she craves right now. "Okay, Addy. I understand. We're friends. I hope you understand that I'm here to protect you and London from anything and anyone. Do you understand that?" He asks her, and she can see that he means it. Wholeheartedly, he will be their protector.

"I understand," Addison whispers out. She noticed he called her by a new nickname, and she likes it, a lot.

"I'm going for a walk in the woods. Are you two going to be okay while I'm gone?" He stands, increasing the distance between them.

Addison nods and looks up at him, wiping her tears away. "Yes, we'll be fine. Thanks."

He nods, and cradles her cheeks in both his hands, kisses her forehead and then releases her. He turns, and without another word, he walks out the back door. Addison hears the door shut behind him and she knows her and London are alone.

She sits on the sofa next to where London has been playing with her toys and whooshes out the breath she didn't know she was holding.

Parker is so intense. So much larger than life. He's her protector. He makes her feel safe, treasured, and…loved?

Maybe…

Chapter Eight

"D<small>AMMIT</small>!" P<small>ARKER YELLS</small> out loud. That's the hardest thing he's ever done. Kissing Addison and then walking away from her. Smelling her personal scent, flowery, like spring, almost, something fresh. Wanting to kiss her, taste her sweet lips, to pull her to him, make love to her. He needs to make her his in every way, but she keeps pushing him away. His cat is frustrated, too, pacing inside him, fighting to get out. He wanted to claim her right then and there.

One day, one day very soon, she will be his. She already owns him in every way possible. She just doesn't know it yet.

He's trying to protect her, and she pushes him away. He understands her need to be strong, but he sees that scared little thing of a woman and he can't help it. He *needs* to protect her. His leopard wants to go all alpha male on her. Show her she belongs to them.

Parker walks into the woods on the path he's taken for many years now. Worn into the ground of short grasses and trees. He's walked this path forever since he was a child first shifting. He goes deeper into the cover of the trees, making sure he's far enough in that Addison won't hear or see him change.

He allows his leopard to stretch out and take over his human body. The fur comes out in black silkiness. His claws pointed and sharp. A loud snarl travels from deep down low in his gut, making its way up and out his mouth.

When he shifts slowly, his clothes stay on him, in human form. He likes to undress and stash his clothes, just in case something happens, he'll still have clothing to dress into when he goes back into human form.

The leopard has taken over and stretches out, extending his claws on a nearby tree. Shaking out his fur, he starts to trot through the woods. Not running today, just a nice jog to help loosen up the muscles. To help clear his head.

Parker lets his leopard take over the run a bit then slows it back to a jog. Coming down to the river's edge on his property, he laps up the cool water. He gets a strange feeling in his gut suddenly. Like he's being watched, or something is wrong. He lifts his head, licking the water droplets off his muzzle.

Looking around, he lifts his nose to the air. His ears perk on full alert. Nothing in the woods, nothing around him that he can sense, yet. He feels like his skin is crawling. He catches a familiar aroma in the air. *Evil. Pure evil.*

Running full tilt, chasing the nauseating scent, he finally comes up to the road leading towards his home. The smell here is stronger. A black truck sits on the side of the road. He slowly and cautiously walks over to it, watching and sniffing around, cautious of what's around him.

The vehicle is warm when Parker leans his side against it, but no human is in it or around it, and he doesn't smell a human anywhere nearby. There, he catches it. They've entered the woods on foot. One person, a man.

Parker is a mile from his home and the demon has become the hunter once again, searching for Addison. He snarls and growls as he runs back into the woods, racing towards home. It's late afternoon, according to the sun sitting lower in the sky and he's been gone for a few hours. He's anxious, not knowing what he'll find when he gets there.

Parker stops on the border of the woods near the house. He can smell Derek, but he's not here. Parker has missed him, and he can tell that Derek didn't go up to the house. Parker hides in the underbrush and shifts back into his human body, thankful for his slow shift earlier and returning clothed this time in his human form.

Parker walks at a fast pace up to the house but trying to appear casual in case Addison is watching. He sniffs the air again. Derek didn't come this close to the house. He stayed back in the cover of the underbrush. *Coward.*

Parker is grateful the jerk chose to stay back this time, without him here to protect Addison and London. Next time he may not be so lucky.

Parker decides he's going to have to stay closer to the house next time he shifts, or even get Addison some kind of an alarm system to let Parker know that there's danger, just in case. He doesn't know of anything he can give her, but perhaps if he contacts the bear shifters or wolf shifters in the area, they might have an idea.

As Parker runs up to the front porch, he takes a deep, calming breath. Letting it out slowly, he lets himself in through the front door. He finds London and Addison asleep on the sofa, and steps quietly into the kitchen.

Glancing at the clock and realizing it's almost four in the afternoon, Parker walks up to his room. He needs to make that call to the bear shifters who live on the other side of town to ask for help.

"Well, well, well. Haven't heard from you in a long time. What's up, cat?" The man on the line, one of Parker's oldest friends' answers.

"Hello, Max. Sorry it's been so long. I need some help, or at least advice."

"Wow, and you're asking me?" Max chuckles. "Okay then. Good luck with that! What's up?"

Parker tells him the short version of the story on how he found Addison and London, and about the fiend who hunts them.

"Holy shit, man! That's a crazy story. How could a man beat up on any woman?" The disgust is evident in Max's voice, even over the phone.

"I don't know, and I need to take care of this situation. I need to know if there's something I can give Addison as protection, something to let me know as a warning while I go for my runs."

"Hmm, I may have something for you." Max says, and they chat for a few minutes coming up with a plan.

A few minutes later, they hang up with a new idea in Parker's mind. Only one solution will take care of the problem and Addison can't be around to see it. It would scare her away from him too damn much at this point. Parker wants to bring her closer and not be afraid of his leopard.

Parker goes back down the stairs and tenderly wakes Addison with a palm to her shoulder, careful not to startle her and upset the sleeping child on her chest.

London lifts her sleepy head from Addison's chest and smiles when she finally focuses on him.

"Hey there, pretty girl. Did you have a good nap?" Parker looks to Addison and then London, "And you, too, London. Did you sleep well?" He grins.

Addison chuckles and Parker lifts London from her chest as the child sits up, arms extended to him.

"I'll go change her diaper quick. Do you want to go to town for dinner tonight?" Parker asks Addison as she wipes the sleep from her eyes.

"Sure. Let me go wash my face and brush my hair. I'm sure I look frightening right about now." She laughs at her own joke.

"You look beautiful, Addison."

She gives him a small smile and Parker follows her to the master bedroom. She walks into the bathroom as he lays London down on the bed to change her.

Parker sets London on the floor after she's changed so she can see her mom in the bathroom, and he goes to throw the diaper away in the kitchen garbage.

Moments later, Addison walks out into the living room with London on her hip and the backpack over her shoulder. "We're ready when you are." She announces.

It's starting to get warmer outside with summer coming so they decide to forgo jackets.

Excited to get the two of them out of the house, Parker drives them into the town of Camas Valley, about twenty minutes away, keeping the conversation light and happy all the way there. He's determined that Addison enjoy the evening out.

***

By the time they're seated in the diner, it's almost six.

Addison hands London some saltine crackers and the child shoves them into her mouth, cracking them into crumbles and making both Addison and Parker laugh at her antics. The child flashes them a grin, shoves a few smaller pieces into her mouth and then grabs her bottle of milk.

During dinner, Parker and Addison have easy conversation and he reminds her that she has to call her sister. She laughs nervously at the reminder and says she'll call her when they get home.

Suddenly, Parker catches a familiar scent drifting in as the bell above the door chimes. His back stiffens as he looks up behind Addison, catching sight of a greaseball in dirty jeans and a ripped jacket. He keeps his face stoic, not wanting to alarm Addison.

The demon has arrived.

***

Sitting here in the smaller booth, watching Parker eat his burger, Addison can't take her eyes off his mouth. Nice full lips. Strong jaw line. Piercing blue eyes. Straight nose.

Parker is too good to be true. All raw male and alpha. *He'd be a great husband for some lucky woman. Too bad it couldn't be me. I have too much baggage. And then there's London. An added bonus for me but extra baggage for any man.*

Addison is feeding London a few of the crackers and a handful of cereal as she hears the bell chime above the door. It's a constant ringing, dinging. This place is busy and the food you get for the price is a good deal. No wonder they're busy.

But this time, Addison sees Parker freeze, just a second, and then he relaxes. Okay, that was weird. She can feel the hairs on the back of her neck raise and a chill runs over her arms. Must be a breeze from the door opening constantly.

Parker chews his food and sets down his huge burger. He takes a sip from his lemonade, his gaze directed behind Addison at the customers walking in and out.

After their appetites are sated, and London has made a mess on the floor, Parker sits back and appears relaxed, continuing the idle chit chat. She tells him she needs to check London's diaper and he gets up from the table with her, following behind them to the restroom. *Okay, that's weird. He's never done that before.*

"I'll wait right here for you," Parker says, looking straight into her eyes as he settles his back against the wall, arms crossed over his chest. She gives him a sideways look but shrugs and makes her way into the ladies' room.

The child changed and cleaned, Addison walks out of the restroom with London on her hip and the backpack over her shoulder, meeting Parker at the restroom door. He looks stressed, and angry.

"Come on, let's get out of here." He puts his hand on her lower back, guiding her toward the door and their table. He takes London from Addison, holding her close to him, and without stopping on his way to the door, drops two twenties on the table.

Parker quickly leads the way to his truck, helping Addison up and shutting her door. He buckles London into her seat, and slams the door, walking quickly around the front of his truck. He scans the parking lot and then climbs in to the drivers' seat.

Turning the key in the ignition, he shifts into reverse and guns the engine, backing the truck out of the parking spot, making Addison nervous. He's still looking around. For whom or what Addison doesn't know. As Parker drives them out of town, Addison can see a black truck, a very familiar black truck, sitting at the gas station on the edge of town. There's a man pumping gas, leaning against it. The man looks up as they drive by.

It's Derek. He's found them.

Chapter Nine

PARKER'S BEEN WATCHING Addison for any reaction as he's been driving toward home. He knew Derek saw Addison and London in the diner with him, but he didn't approach them. Lucky for him. He just smiled his evil smile at Parker and walked out.

Addison had seemed fine, unaware of the danger, but then Addison stiffened in her seat when they drove by the gas station and Parker knew she'd seen him standing there, that evil smirk of his plastered across his face.

Parker hit the gas, heading toward home. His own territory, where he could protect them easier.

Addison hadn't said anything the whole drive home, but when Parker drove up to the house she opened her door, unbuckling her seatbelt and sliding down to the ground in one fast, fluid movement.

"Addison, please, wait for me to help you."

He puts the truck in park and grabs the keys, sliding out his door and running around the truck.

She's already up in the backseat unclipping a sleeping London and pulling her from the truck. Parker grabs Addison by the hips so she doesn't fall backwards with the baby and she screams, surprised at the contact and terrified of the hands on her body.

"Addison, it's just me, baby. I've got you. I didn't want you falling out of the truck with London in your arms." He eases her down to the ground and once she's steady, she jogs to the house with a now very awake London in her arms.

He grabs the backpack from the back seat and locks up the truck.

Once inside, he locks the front door and sets his keys on the kitchen table. Addison is not in the kitchen or living room. She's turned on a light here and there, so she doesn't bump into things, but Parker knows she's hiding in the bedroom.

When he gets there, he can see London is awake and sitting on the floor, playing with a few toys. He can hear Addison in the bathroom, clinking things around.

She walks out of the bathroom carrying her toiletries as he sits on the bed. She's packing to leave. She's running. Again. She's allowing that jackass to scare her and he wins, again.

"What are you doing, Addison? Talk to me, please." Parker is watching her race around the room like a small tornado, cleaning up her and London's belongings and packing them up as fast as she can. She's become comfortable in the short time she's been living here.

"I'm packing our things. He's found us and it's only a matter of time until he finds out we live here with you, and he comes for us. We need to leave before that happens. He will kill us, Parker.

Do you understand that? He will kill us both." Addison almost yells the last part.

She's upset, angry, and determined to leave. He can see the resolve in her eyes. He knows she believes that Derek will kill her, but she doesn't know what Parker and his leopard are capable of. Whether he's a man or beast. He's lethal. In all senses of the word.

Parker walks up behind her and as she stands up, he wraps his arms around her waist, pulling her back into his chest.

"Addison, it's okay. Relax. Please, you've got to trust me to keep you and London safe. He won't hurt either of you while you're with me. I can and will protect you. Nothing he does will hurt me. I promise."

Addison sags against him and then turns in his arms to face him. "Parker, you leave for long walks in the woods or you stay in the house with us constantly. I can't keep you in the house or on protective duty twenty-four hours a day, seven days a week until he decides to come for us. I don't want to hide from him. I want to face my fear. Let him know I'm no longer afraid of him. I want you in my corner. I'm not big or strong enough to fight him, but if I have you with me, I know we'll be okay." She traces her palm over Parker's cheek and down to his jaw. "I just want to say my piece to the demon before I'm done with him." She says more fiercely.

"Addison, you've become such a brave, strong woman. I love that you want to protect London. I love that you want to stand up to that monster of a man. I'm so proud of you. I hope London becomes just like you. You're a great mom to her." Parker touches the lock of hair that's come loose and pulls it behind her ear. "I just hope that one day, you find a great dad for her as well." Parker looks her straight in the eyes, hoping she's catching his meaning.

In the short time that Parker has known Addison, he's been slowly falling for her. Not that he could help it. His leopard has been panting after her since they first saw her in the crumpled car. She's everything he wants in a mate, in a lover, in a wife.

Hailey was a great lover and wife, and soon to be mother. She would have been a great mom to their unborn daughter. They were excited for their firstborn. Hailey was his mate, but there's more with Addison.

Now, here, with Addison and London, Parker has a pre-made family. Although, making more babies with Addison would be the best thing ever. Her body was made for having babies. Her personality. Her beauty. Her protective nature and nurturing of London is already there.

Parker pulls Addison to sit on the edge of the bed with him. He has her cool, shaking hands grasped in his.

Addison is terrified, and she should be, but Parker is here and she's safe. He's told her that repeatedly. But the one thing she doesn't know, yet, is how safe she really is.

He sits there, staring into her eyes, wiping a tear that has fallen down her cheek with his thumb. She looks up into his eyes, her gaze searching.

Finally, Addison nods and then leans into Parker's chest, allowing him to pull her into him. To comfort her, to make her feel protected and safe. This here…this is her finally, fully trusting Parker, and he's overjoyed with happiness. She's come to him for comfort.

She breathes deep and her body relaxes a little. He holds her, playing with the ends of her hair, softly. Tugging gently every so often.

They just sit together on the edge of the bed, holding each other. Breathing each other in. Comforting each other. He knows she's scared. She knows he's angry at the situation. She knows he will fight Derek to protect her and London with his life. He knows he will win her heart in the end.

After what seems like a lifetime of holding each other, Addison slowly eases back from Parker's arms.

"I'm going to get London ready for bed. She's getting tired." Addison finally speaks.

Parker notices London rubbing her eyes and nods his agreement. "Okay. Do you want to come back out in the living room when you're done? We could watch a movie together, or maybe talk a bit if you're up to it?"

They've both made progress in trusting and sharing what's happening, and Parker needs more information on Derek. Although he's loathing to ask her about it now, there's really little choice with the guy closing in on them. He wants to know what Derek is capable of, other than beating women. Does he own any weapons of any kind? Parker wants to be prepared.

Addison nods her head and says, "That sounds good. I'll meet you in the living room once I get London to bed, okay?"

"Sure. I'll get us some popcorn and water, if that's okay, too? Any kind of movie, or do you want to watch something specific?".

"Whatever you want. Nothing scary, though, please. And popcorn sounds great." Addison smiles and seems unexpectedly happy.

Parker stands up from the bed and leans over Addison, cupping the back of her head and kissing her forehead. He turns toward the kitchen, leaving her to take care of putting London to bed.

Parker steps out into the kitchen and starts the popcorn. Walking over to the television, he presses the power button and the screen flickers to life. He's flipping through a few channels, looking for a movie. Something neutral they could both enjoy.

Hearing the popcorn slow down on popping, he jogs to the microwave, plucking the bag out quickly before it burns. Pouring the popcorn into a bowl and grabbing two water bottles from the fridge, he walks back into the living room. A minute later, Addison joins him. They both sit on the couch and Parker hands her a water.

"Thanks. So, what movie did you find for us to watch?" She asks.

"Umm...I'm not sure what you're in the mood for." He glances over to her face as he says it, not meaning anything sexual, but he can see a little heat in Addison's eyes.

"I could watch anything, really. Nothing sappy or scary. Do you have that one movie where people get stuck in the snowstorm of the century? It's where they're in a New York library and the one kid's dad saves them by trekking across the US in fifty feet of snow or whatever? I don't remember the name."

Parker watches her face light up as she describes this movie she likes.

"Yeah," Parker chuckles, "I think I have that one. Hold on, I'll put it on."

Parker flicks a button on the remote and turns out the lights. He grabs a blanket from the back of the couch, and drapes it over their legs, setting the big bowl of popcorn on their laps, and presses play.

As the movie starts, Addison scoots closer to Parker, and she snuggles in as he lifts his arm up and across her shoulders. "This is the right movie, thank you."

"No problem, Addy. Now, let's watch it, I like this one, too."

***

Addison has been slowly inching closer to Parker throughout the movie, basically climbing almost into his lap.

Parker moves the popcorn bowl and sets it on the side table, the water bottles are on the coffee table in front of them.

He lifts his feet and rests them on the coffee table, skootching down into the couch more, removing his arm from around her shoulders.

He reaches for her hand and links their fingers together, leaning his head toward hers.

Addison tips her head up and looks into Parker's eyes, then down to his lips, licking her own.

"Addison, can I kiss you?" He whispers, a low and sexy tone.

"Yes." Her answer is so quiet.

He heard it but only due to his better animal hearing. He glances at her lips, then his gaze drifts to her eyes, confirming her words.

She tips her head slightly, her movements encouraging.

Knowing that's all the invitation he needs, Parker brushes his lips across her slightly open mouth.

He flicks his tongue across her lips lightly tasting her. His inner cat is purring and pushing for more. Wanting to claim her as their mate. Parker ignores his cat and turns his body slightly toward Addison.

Just teasing and tasting her with his tongue and lips. Taking his time. Not wanting to move too fast. He slips his tongue out and licks her lips more, and he can hear her breathing get heavier. He presses his lips to hers and slowly, ever so softly, claims her lips as his.

There's no turning back. Addison is his. He knows it now. He's never felt this...melding of souls before. Of becoming one. Of becoming whole with just a kiss. She's his, and forever will be from here on out.

For some reason, Parker knows he was meant to find Addison and London that night. It's the stars aligning, or fate or karma or something that made everything come together and he found his everlasting love. Yes, this is what this is...love. Love for Addison. He loves Addison with everything he is and everything he will become. For eternity.

Addison is his one true soul mate.

***

Addison can feel Parker's tongue slide across her lips, wetting them and she's anticipating more. Her whole body is vibrating in anticipation. She can hear a faint growling or purring coming from Parker's chest. Oh, so sexy.

She slides her hand to the back of his head, holding her to him, and he does the same to her, claiming her lips fully. No more teasing and wetting of the lips, this is a full-on contact.

Parker lifts her so she's straddling his lap. He moves his hands to cup her cheeks, holding her face to his.

Addison tangles her fingers in his soft hair. She is on fire, hot and needy. She can feel it deep in her belly, in her core. She wants Parker. Now. She hasn't been turned on like this, ever.

Lust and hunger like this for another person sexually and sensually can only be explained as animalistic.

She can feel her core tingling as she slowly grinds her pelvis on Parker's lap, increasingly frustrated with the stupid blanket bunched between them and in the way of what she needs.

Parker must be seeking the same thing because he pulls the blanket away in haste, and now their bodies are only separated by their jeans between them. She grinds on his jeans right where she needs him, and he shifts just slightly to give her that little bit more.

Addison can feel his need for her, centering at her core, rubbing and grinding on her, just in the spot she needs. Her breathing has become labored, and she's close.

Parker moves his hand behind her lower back, pulling her toward him, helping her push and grind herself on him.

Addison moans and makes a quiet cry to the heavens above. Parker lets go of her head and grips her hips harder, helping her thrust against his covered erection. Her hands grip his jaw line and she gives herself over to him with a cry, despite the clothing between them.

***

Parker is so hot and ready to release inside of his jeans. He pushes her back just a bit more and he reaches down inside of his jeans, gripping himself, willing himself not to come like an adolescent teen dry humping his first girlfriend on his parents couch.

"Addison, I have to stop. I'm gonna come in my jeans if you don't stop. Oh…God." Parker moans, breathing heavily.

"Parker, I need to have you, please." She whimpers in his ear, her tongue flicking out to trace the shell of his ear.

He lifts his hips off the couch, shoving down his jeans and boxers.

Addison sits up and pulls off her jeans, leaving her panties on.

"Honey, wait...I don't have a condom in the house, are you on anything?" In desperation, Parker prays she is.

"Yes, I am on the pill. Please, Parker, don't make me wait any longer." She whimpers, and her hands are frantic over his shirt-covered chest.

"Thank you," is all he can say before he lifts Addison's shirt over her head and drops it to the floor. He unclasps her bra, pulling it off as she lifts his shirt over his head between the kissing and touching.

When all clothes are on the floor, he lifts Addison back onto his lap, straddling him once again.

She grabs his cock in her hands, she uses the wetness that has formed on the tip to lubricate her hands and slowly moves them up and down his shaft.

Parker groans loudly. "Addison stop, I have to be inside you when I come. Please, let me. I have to have you." Parker pleads with her.

Addison ends his torture and sits up, then slowly lowers her body on his, taking him inside of her inch by agonizing inch. They both groan loudly as their two bodies become one.

The extreme need for Parker to claim Addison as his soul mate is overwhelming as soon as he's settled deep within her. His cat is clawing on the inside, wanting to claim, to mate, and to make her his. *Claim her! Bite her neck!* The cat hisses.

Parker pulls Addy closer to his chest, skin to skin and he watches her breasts squish against his chest. Beautiful, full globes of flesh and he wants to taste them.

Addison is wiggling and struggling to move, to make the friction she desperately needs to find her release, but Parker holds her still.

"Addison, let me love you, babe. Let me savor you. I'll let you come, baby, but let me taste you for a while." He whispers to her.

She looks at him, seeing the desperation in his eyes, she tries to hold back. "Parker, I need to come, please. It's right there."

Parker holds onto her waist tightly and leans his head onto her collarbone. Addison wraps her arms around his neck and head. Parker slowly lifts and drops Addison's body on to his.

He can feel the fluttering of her inner muscles and knows she's close. Faster and faster he lifts and drops, lifts and drops, and finally, Addison screams out into the dark room her release. "Parker!"

Parker quickly grabs her head and claims her mouth to his, silencing her scream, taking it into his body. Her whole body is trembling on top of his.

He can feel her inner muscles tightening and releasing around his cock. He can't stop the tingling feeling. He lets it send him over the edge, his own climax chasing right after hers. He shouts out his release, "Oh! Addison!"

Parker's orgasm sends Addison on another release. Not as high as the first one, he's sure, but damn near close.

Calming now, she leans her exhausted, weary body against Parker's chest and falls asleep. Exhausted and sated.

Parker feels his manhood slip from within her. He slowly lifts her, cradling her to his chest, and carries her to her bedroom, being quiet to not wake up London.

Now the decision: to lie with her or leave her alone to sleep?

He goes back to grab his boxers, pulling them on, and shuts off the television. He comes back into the bedroom and quietly lies next to Addison, covering them both up for the night. Parker pulls Addison into his chest, she plops an arm around his ribs, her leg going up on his hip. A sign of a sexually sedated woman.

He breathes out a huff and sighs in relief. He falls asleep a few minutes later, Addison wrapped in his arms. Parker's last thought is that she's trusted him with her memories, her mind. She now trusted him with her body.

Next...her heart and love.

Chapter Ten

ADDISON WAKES UP with a start and she's confused. Her body aches, and she's in her bed. The body aches are from a wonderful night of making love with Parker. She's never been so well loved before and she's basking in the afterglow. She's used to being sore, but this is an amazing, good kind of sore.

She's lying on her side and she can feel a warm, strong, male body behind her. Parker. He stayed with her and slept with her. His arm resting under her breasts, tight around her ribs, and he's spooned right behind her. His breath is blowing her hair across her cheek, and she can feel a morning surprise growing against her lower back.

It's just starting to get light in the room from the sun rising. She pulls from Parker's arms slowly, not wanting to wake him, and glancing at London still asleep in her crib, she walks into the bathroom, shutting the door quietly behind her.

Turning on the shower and waiting for it to warm, she takes care of her morning needs and cleans up from her love making session with Parker. When she's finished, she gets into the warm rush of the water of the shower. Allowing the water to fall down her head, neck, shoulders, and the rest of her body.

She's still nervous because Derek knows that she's with Parker. He could be looking for him, then find her. He could be asking around to find out where they are. Or he could follow them home.

Home. Home is with Parker. Derek was never home. He was hell. Parker thoroughly loved her last night and was very giving to her needs. A protector of her. Even while he was making love to her, he had her wrapped up in his arms.

God, last night was the most sensual time she can remember. She lost her virginity at seventeen and didn't sleep around but had a total of four men she slept with, including Parker. Parker. He's definitely someone she wants to keep around.

Thinking about him now, she's picturing what they did last night. Her breathing becomes heavier, and her hands drift up to her breasts. Slowly thumbing over her nipples, pulling them, then lightly pinching them into tight, twin peaks.

Leaning against the shower wall, she glides her hand down her soft stomach, to her secret depths. Wet from the shower, and an active sexual mind, she pushes a finger in, then out.

A few minutes of this and her breathing is louder and heavier. Her inner muscles are starting to quiver and clench. She clasps a palm over her mouth as she's thinking of Parker, she reaches her quiet release.

After her climax, she washes and rinses her hair and body. She steps from the shower grabbing the nearest towel, wrapping it around her body, then she reaches for another for her hair. There's a soft knock at the bathroom door.

"Come in." She answers, knowing it's Parker.

The door opens, and Parker peeks his head in, "London woke up and I changed her diaper. She leaked through, so I cleaned her up as best I could and dressed her. I haven't been able to strip her bed yet or feed her."

"Oh! Thank you. Give me a minute and I'll be right there to take care of her," she replies quickly.

Parker opens the door fully and caresses Addison's cheek with the back of his knuckles. "Addy, I've got this. She's fine. Just dry off and get dressed. She'll be okay for a few minutes, or until you're ready."

Addison looks up to Parker's eyes and he smiles at her, reassuring her. *He's got this, I can trust him. It's okay.*

Parker walks out after kissing Addison on the nose and shuts the door behind him. She quickly dries off and puts on, panties, bra, jeans, and a tee shirt. Quickly towel drying her hair, brushing it out straight, she whips it up into a ponytail.

Grabbing a pair of socks, she walks out into the living room where Parker sits on the floor with London, who's standing, gripping Parker's shirt for balance.

Addison sits on the couch next to them and pulls on her socks. She rests her chin in her palm, watching the two interact, and she likes the image.

She can see London is being taken care of. Addison's being taken care of, too. Emotionally, physically, financially, and now sexually. And she feels safe.

Parker looks up to Addison from where he's sitting on the floor, then moves to sit next to her on the couch.

"How are you this morning? I hope you slept well." He gives her a slight smirk. "London was starting to wake up and I didn't want to disturb you in the shower. Hope you don't mind me taking her out here." Parker asks, holding her hand in his and gently rubbing her knuckles with his thumb.

How could she mind Parker taking care of London? "No, of course not, I don't mind. Thank you for being so considerate. I've never really had a good night's sleep like I did last night." She blushes as the words come out of her mouth, knowing why she slept so well.

Parker puts his arm around her and pulls her close. "You were sleeping quite soundly last night." He leans back from Addison and smiles at her. His inner cat purring quietly.

"I'm going for a run in the woods soon, you two going to be okay for a few hours?" Parker asks Addison cautiously.

"Yeah, I think we could find something to do around here while you're gone. Will you be home for dinner?" She asks.

"I'll be home after lunch, but before dinner. Feel free to look around in the freezer for something, or I can cook when I get back. Your choice. Have you had venison before?" He asks her quietly, his breath tickling her ear.

"No, I haven't."

Parker looks to the clock on the wall, noticing it's almost ten. "I'll go for a run and I'll be back soon. Maybe around three or so? Then I'll help you with dinner."

"That's kind of a really long run. Are you going to be okay running for that long?"

"I don't run the whole time. Plus, there's a river and a few streams to bounce around in. Maybe I'll have to take you to them when it gets a bit warmer and London can enjoy it, too. It's quite beautiful there."

"Okay, sounds good. I guess we'll see you in a few hours." Addison squeezes his hand in hers.

Parker gets up, kisses her on the lips, and then heads out the back door. He locked the front door last night, so he knows that's secure. As he gets outside, he scents the air. Just in case. He turns, and locks then shuts the back door behind him. He worries about his girls in the house while he's gone.

His girls. He likes the sound of that.

Entering the woods, he walks the path for a while in his human form, thinking. After a few minutes, he can see the small shack about one hundred feet in front of him. It's been here forever, and he quickly goes in and strips out of his clothes.

It used to be an old shed but he converted it into a small shack, keeping hidden well into the woods just for this. The old outhouse was closer to the house, but he tore it down a few years back.

He eases out of the small building, pushing the door closed, and letting his human form be taken over by his leopard. Easing down to all fours, his leopard is complete in moments.

As Parker's leopard stretches out the animal muscles, this gives him time to think of last night, making love to Addy. He listened to her this morning taking her shower, the little noises she made in there as he lifted London from her crib.

His overly sensitive ears hearing her moan as he shut the bedroom door behind him, trying to block some of the sounds coming from in there. He wanted to go in and shower with her, help her pleasure herself in there. But knowing he couldn't leave London alone, he stayed in the living room. Achingly hard and aroused.

The images go flipping through Parker's head as his cat takes the lead, running through the woods. A big splash of water hitting him in the face, snaps him out of his thoughts of Addison.

Hey, you're supposed to be paying attention here with me, not floating in the back ground like a backseat passenger. Parker's leopard growls.

I know, I'm sorry. She's just got me in knots. I love her but I'm so afraid of scaring her when she finds out about us. I don't want her to run.

She won't run if you tell her and then show her. Be easy on her. She's our mate, she'll accept us both for who we are.

I know. I just don't want to lose her. Parker replies.

His cat continues through the woods, sometimes running, sometimes walking. They get down to the river, lapping up the cool water, then decide to head back home.

Home...that's where his future lies. Home with Addison and London. His cat picks up the pace and is eager to see her again. To hold her again. Addison.

***

Back at the house, Addison figures she can clean the bathroom and the kitchen. Then she can tackle the pile of growing dirty clothes to be washed. Since Parker is out for his run, for a few hours, whatever that entails. Who even runs that far and back?

It's just after two in the afternoon and London is sleeping in her crib, lunch is cleaned up, clothes washed, dried and put away and the house is cleaned as well. She sits down on the couch and flips on the television to waste some time until Parker comes back.

A few minutes later, Addison hears a vehicle come down the drive and flips the power to the TV screen off. She gets up and walks to the big bay window and glances around through the gauzy curtains. She can see a big black truck coming to a stop in front of the house and a familiar man in the front driver's seat.

Derek.

She gasps, and steps away from the window. She quickly checks the lock on the door and then runs quietly into her room, shutting that door with a soft click. She sits on her bed, with her knees tucked up tight to her chest and biting her thumbnail. Praying that London stays asleep.

Knock. Knock. Knock.

Ten seconds pass.

Knock, knock, knock. His fist on the front door again.

Addison cringes even more, pressing her back into the headboard of the bed. She can hear muffled voices coming from outside now and she runs to her door wondering who it is. Quickly unlocking the bedroom door then running to the front door, unlocking that, too.

Addison listens to the voices outside and makes out that it's Derek… and Parker…

"Yeah, well, this is my property and I'm asking nicely for you to leave." She hears Parker.

"Yeah, well, you have *my* property in that fucking house and I want it back. It's mine!" Derek yells at Parker.

"Listen, fucknut, I don't know what planet you came from, but here in Oregon, people are not property. They are human beings and we treat our women with respect. You got that, asshole?" Parker is trying to keep calm.

Addison opens the door and Derek turns to her.

"Addison, get your fat fucking ass out here and in the fucking truck, now! Stop being a whore and get out here! You're mine and I own you, bitch!"

Parker shoves Derek off the front porch and pushes him all the way to his truck, away from Addy.

Derek is stumbling and tripping backward the whole way.

"Listen here you piece of shit, if I *ever* hear you or smell your rotten stench again, I will kill you, do you hear me, dickhead?" Parker says heatedly, but calmly.

"You and what army? You're pussy-whipped from her, aren't you? You're a cunt! That's my pussy and I'm coming back for it. Stay out of my way, she's mine, and I'm coming back to get my property. You can have the fucking kid and do whatever with her, she just gets in my way."

Derek yells in Parker's face and has been pointing a grimy finger in Addison's direction.

"Don't even think of it. I'll kill you before you get onto my property." Parker talks in a low, deadly voice. Addison can just barely hear him from the edge of the front porch.

"Just wait, you fuck, I'm gonna kick your ass so bad, and then I'll make you watch me fuck Addison's ass. Not like I haven't done that before. And she takes it so well. She loooovvves it!" Derek snarls and looks over to Addison.

Parker grabs the front of Derek's shirt and slams him up against his truck. "You're a fucking asshole and I'll put your ass six feet under before you can blink. Don't ever talk about Addy like that again, you hear me? Or I'll kill you right in front of her. You've lost her. I've claimed her. She's mine because she wants to be, not because I'm making the choice for her." He yells in Derek's face.

Addison can't believe what she just heard. *'You've lost her. I've claimed her. She's mine because she wants to be, not because I'm making the choice for her.'* Those words just came from Parker. *'I've claimed her.'*

Claimed her? I haven't been claimed. What does that mean? This isn't some kind of an animal mating ritual.

She continues to watch the argument between the two men and hopes Derek leaves soon. He has no business being here. Parker's right. She doesn't belong to him anymore. She never belonged to anyone. She's her own person.

"Get out of here, Derek. You're not welcome here!" Addison shouts at Derek before she thinks about saying it, crossing her arms over her chest.

"Shut your fucking mouth, little girl, before I fill it for you!" Derek points at her.

Parker grabs Derek again by his shirt, pulls him away from the truck, opens the door and practically lifts him up into it, slamming the door behind him.

"Get the fuck out of here or I swear I will kill you right here, right now!" Parker screams at Derek. Just barely holding his leopard in from bursting out at the seams and tearing the fucker into shreds.

Derek starts the truck, backs up, and then floors it down the long driveway, ripping up rocks and pebbles, throwing them back at Parker. As he's driving out of sight, Derek flips them the middle finger out the window as a goodbye gesture.

Parker looks up to Addison, his hands resting on his hips. Her face is ghostly white, and she looks like she's going to pass out. Parker runs up to her on the front porch and cradles her in an embrace before she can fall to the floor or passes out.

"Addy, are you okay, honey? Do you need to sit down?" He's clearly worried about her over this ordeal.

"Parker, I spouted off to him. I've angered him even more. He knows I'm here with London and he'll be back for me. He won't stop until he gets me back or kills me, I'm sure of it. Or he'll do something to London just to hurt me. I can't even think of what he would do to her." Clearly in panic mode, Addison breaks down crying and trembling in Parker's thick, strong arms.

Parker walks her into the house and shuts the door behind them. Walking her over to the couch, they both sit down, holding each other.

A moment later, London shouts out, letting them know that she's now awake. Now that she's up, Parker can't really comfort Addy like he wants to. Nothing sexually, just to give her soft touches and gentle kisses.

Addison starts to get up and Parker says, "No, stay here. I'll get her." He softly kisses her on the forehead.

While Parker is getting London from her crib and changing her diaper, he breathes deep to release the tension of the moments that just passed. Releasing that tension before he's with his girls. No negativity from that asshole.

He breathes deep once again and then grins at London standing up, her hands on his shoulders balancing while he pulls her cotton pants up over her diapered butt.

Sliding his hands under her armpits, and hoisting her on his hip, he leaves the bedroom and enters the living room. He quickly glances at the clock, almost dinnertime.

He sets London on the floor and asks Addy if she's hungry.

"I'm hungry, yes. I'm sorry, but I forgot to take something out for dinner. I cleaned your house while you were out running."

"I saw that when I came in. Thank you. You didn't need to do that. Let me grab a quick shower and we can go out, if you're up to it?" He asks.

"Sure, I'm going to go wash my face and I can be ready in a few minutes." She gets up and pulls London from the floor.

Parker walks up to Addison and pulls her closer to his chest, rubbing his hands over her back and shoulders.

"It's going to be okay, Addy. He won't do you or London any harm. Do you trust me to keep you both safe?"

"Yes, Parker. I do trust you. I'm just afraid that Derek will come back and hurt you or take

180

London from us." She expresses her concern. Not about her, but for him and her daughter.

"Addy, I want to talk to you, but not with London here. Let's go to dinner and when we put her to bed later, we can talk." Parker cups his hand over her cheek, and leans in to kiss her lips, softly.

London giggles and pats his cheek.

Parker pats her hand with his and turns to go upstairs to take his shower.

Addison goes into her bathroom, setting London on the floor with toys while she washes her face free of the tears. Addison can hear the shower turn on and knows Parker's naked.

She didn't really get to see him in all his glory last night, but if and when the next time comes, she's going to look, learn and lick every flat, muscular dip and plane of his body.

Just thinking back to Parker making love to her, heats her up again. She washes her face in cooler water and eases the heat rushing over her cheeks.

She pats her face dry with the towel and then walks back into the bedroom. She quickly packs a small bag for London and then picks her up from the floor, walking back to the living room to wait for Parker.

Waiting for Parker isn't a problem. He's worth waiting for.

Chapter Eleven

THEY GET INTO Parker's truck and he drives them into town. He is searching around for the asshole that decided to grace them with his presence earlier. Parker can't see his truck anywhere and can only smell little bits of his scent around town.

He can't believe the balls Derek has for showing up on his property and demanding to take back a woman that he never earned the respect for.

He's proud of Addison for standing up to the jerk and can't believe she spoke to him that way.

Parker is so happy she felt empowered and she wasn't afraid. Until Derek left and shot out that last bit of a warning.

As the three of them take their seats at the diner, and London is placed in the high chair,

Parker's been scenting the air and looking around for Derek. So far, so good. No sign of him.

Parker chooses a buffalo burger and fries and Addison chooses a roast beef and cheese sandwich. London gets her usual finger food.

Parker and Addison make good conversation, and he's trying not to think about Derek while they finish their dinner.

On the way home, Parker can scent Derek but can't see where he is. He makes it home safely and gets Addy and London inside, locking the door behind them.

"What was the rush getting us in here?" Addison questions Parker.

"No rush, I just wanted to get inside. Maybe watch a movie?" Parker lies to Addison and feels guilty for it. He isn't one to lie.

"I want to get London in the bath before bed, then we can watch a movie, is that okay? Plus, you wanted to have a talk." Addison reminds him.

"Okay, give her a bath. I should make a phone call. Let me know when you're done. I'll be up in my room." Parker says, distracted by something.

He heads up the stairs to the second floor while Addison takes London into the main floor bathroom and runs some water in the large tub. He can hear London's laughs and giggles as she's bathed, and the little girl is splashing Addison.

Parker walks down the hall to his bedroom, as the call goes through.

"Hello? Wow, I get two calls from you in a month, and nothing for a few years. How sweet!" The voice answers jokingly.

"Max, I need your help. The situation is at its peak and I want back up in the woods in case I'm not here and that asshole comes while I'm running." Parker answers gruffly.

"You haven't gotten rid of the situation yet?" Max questions suddenly getting serious.

"I hadn't found him until the fucker came knocking on my door this afternoon while I was running." Parker informs Max.

"Have you made Addison your mate yet? Then she could defend herself, you know."

"I haven't gotten that far with her. I would love to, but I don't want to scare her either." Parker says.

"I hear you. Is she your true mate? Has your leopard already told you?"

"Yes, she's my soul mate. I can feel it, and my leopard is scratching to get out and claim her as ours." Parker sighs. "I almost lost control this afternoon when Derek was here. The shit that was spewing from his mouth was bad and I just about killed him right there."

"Damn, man. You can't show her by killing a man in front of her!" Max scolds Parker.

"I know! I held back, but he was just saying disrespectful things, talking nasty about her just to push me. I would have shredded him right there if she wasn't there behind me." Parker growls.

Max growls back, "Parker, I've got your back, man. When and where, my friend? When and where?"

Parker tells him about what happened when he got back to the house, with Derek standing on the front porch. He told Max some of the things Derek had said about Abby, and Max and Parker both were growling at that.

By the time Parker and Max end their call, Parker needs a run, but can't because of the promise of talking and a movie with Addison. He needs to calm down. On the promise of friends patrolling on their off time around the house and property, Parker feels better about Addison and London's safety while he runs.

He treks down the stairs to Addison who's waiting on the couch, curled up in the corner with the blanket covering her. She looks up to him when he walks over, and she wipes her eyes of the lingering tears.

"Hey now. What's with the tears?" Parker sits next to her and pulls her to his chest. Encompassing her in his arms.

She's unable to do the same because her arms are trapped under the blanket and she tenses, but then relaxes into Parker.

"I'm just overwhelmed that he's found us, and I'm scared." Addison confesses.

"Addison, I've told you before. I will not let him hurt you or London. You have to believe in me on that, okay?"

Parker sits back from Addison and rubs her arms with his hands. She pulls her arms out from the blanket and sits back into the couch, resting her head on the back-couch cushion.

"Can we have our talk now? I want to ask you some questions and I want to tell you a little about me, is that okay?" Parker asks her cautiously, watching her face.

Looking confused, she nods her head, "Okay. Sure. What do you want to know?"

This is a good thing, Parker thinks. She's open to questions and he can let her know about his leopard a bit at a time before he's forced to show her.

Parker turns to the side and grasps her hands in his. "Well, I want to start on this house and my property." He takes a deep breath in and whooshes it back out. *Here goes nothing.*

She'll be fine. Just ease into the conversation. Tell her about you and your family. About Hailey and your parents. Parker's cat whispers with in his head.

"Okay, so… This house has been in my family for many generations. Each generation added updates, improvements, things like that. Umm… I'm an only child and both of my parents have passed away."

"Oh, Parker, I'm so sorry."

"It's okay. They were traveling and hit ice. Totaled the car. They were both life-lifted by helicopter, but the injuries they sustained were what killed them. Ummm… My grandparents are no longer here either, but I have friends that live close and that is who I called."

"Okay. I have no problem with you calling people, Parker. I understand." Addison squeezes his hands in hers.

Parker looks to Addison's eyes and she's interested in what he's saying to her. *Keep going.* His leopard encourages him.

"I want you to know when Derek comes back to try to take you away with him, he won't succeed, because no matter what he does to me, ever, he won't hurt me. I heal very fast." Parker tries to explain.

"Okay, I know you're protecting London and me. Healing fast. Okay. I'm confused on what you're really trying to tell me here, Parker." Addison sits back, pulling away from him and looking as confused as she professes to be.

Parker lets go of her hands and lets her get more comfortable. He sits back more into the couch cushion, relaxing and looking into her beautiful eyes. He loves her.

"Addison, I want to ask you something. Have you heard of shape shifters?"

Nice! Good way to introduce her. Let her tell you about what she knows about us. The leopard praises him.

"Yes. I read about them in my eBooks'." She replies.

"Okay, well then tell me about those. What have you've read about them?"

"Okay. Well, there are men and women who are human who can change into animals. They're strong. They sometimes live in packs or alone. They're loyal to their mates, and packs and are very protective. They heal very fast and are hard to kill." Addison looks up to Parker's face and it's like a light bulb just went on in her head. She gasps, and her hands fly to her mouth, covering her shock. "Parker…"

"Addison, you're right on all of those facts. Maybe some of those authors are shape shifters as well." Parker eases closer to her.

He knows Addison can't believe what she thinks Parker has just told her, or rather what she's thinking. Parker is a shifter. "Shape shifters aren't real. People write about them in books. They make them up."

Parker says gently, "Addison, did you ever wonder why those authors might know so much about shifters?"

"I don't know. Made them up? Those books are fiction."

Parker looks at her again and he can see the confusion lingering there. Time to fess up and come clean. *Tell her now. She needs to know.* Parker's cat whispers.

"Addison, Shifters are very real in our world. I have friends who are. Family who were." Parker slides his fingers with hers, intertwining them together.

She looks down to their fingers linked together then looks up to his face. Searching for something. The truth? A lie?

"So, what you're saying to me is this…that you're protecting London and me. You heal faster because you're a shifter?" Addison hesitates, then looks at their hands again.

Parker slowly releases a breath. "That's exactly what I'm telling you. Derek can't ever hurt me because I'm a shifter. I need you to believe in me, that I can protect you and London both. I won't get hurt because I can heal very fast."

"So, what? You're a wolf or bear or something inside?"

Parker chuckles, "No, sweetheart. I'm a black leopard. He's been clawing on the inside since we've met you and he's telling me that you're my soul mate. I've fallen in love with you, Addy. Once a shifter finds their mate, there is no one else that they want or need to be with."

"Parker. I'm only a human. How can I be your soul mate?"

"Honey, there are no boundaries or rules when it comes to your soul mate." Parker huffs out a quick breath. "I had another mate and she died many years ago, she was carrying our unborn daughter at the time. Hailey was in her seventh month and she was walking in the woods, blowing off some steam over an argument we had earlier. She was a badger shifter and it was easy to rile her up. She tripped over something, landed on her belly, and hit her head on a rock." Parker's looking to their enjoined fingers and keeps going. "I felt the stab of pain in my head when she fell but didn't quite know where she was. I ran as fast as I could and when I found her, she was unconscious. I picked her up and ran as fast as my human legs could carry her, but she died minutes after I got her back here."

Addison releases her hand from his and she wipes away a stray tear from his cheek. "I'm so sorry, Parker. I didn't know."

"I didn't tell you because I didn't think it mattered. Hailey was my mate, but you are my soul mate. There is no breaking us once we bond, only by death. Addison, I love you and would do anything to protect you and London. She can be my daughter, as well. I love her already." Parker looks at Addison and smiles.

He's such a handsome man. It catches her breath. His blue eyes, dark hair and full physique, so powerful and strong. Now she can see the strength in him. He's her protector. She can now fully understand why she was feeling like there was a darkness in him from the beginning.

Addison takes her hand and touches his cheek, soothing him, from his cheek to his jaw. "I think I love you, too, Parker, but I'm afraid of Derek and what he will do if he knows you and I are together." She looks to their fingers again. "When can you turn into a leopard? Is it anytime or when you get mad? Or…"

"I can change whenever. It happens faster if I'm angry or agitated." He explains.

"So, does it explode out of you or how does it happen?" She's interested now and wants to know more, which is good.

"I'll have to show you sometime soon. I'm going to fight Derek and kill him, Addison. He won't be bothering you ever again. But there's something about him. Do you know if Derek is a shifter?" Parker asks.

"Derek? A shifter? I have no idea. He's never said anything to me. But when he's mad, there have been a few times I thought I've seen his eyes glow or shine or something. But that could have been me. Not seeing things when I was being hit around by him. Or it could have just been him being angry." Addison just plays it off, as if it's no big deal now for her to have been beaten.

"When I scent him, smell him, there's always something off about him. I don't know if he's using something to hide the shifter scent in him or if he just has that scent about him."

"I don't know, Parker. Sorry, I can't be any more help to you there." Addison leans into Parker's chest, resting her palm over his heart.

Parker leans back into the couch and pulls Addison with him and she lies on his chest. She listens to his heart beating and a low rumble within his chest.

She looks up to Parker's face and he smirks, "You can hear that?" A slight blush coming over his cheeks.

"Yes, what is that? Is your leopard purring?" She giggles.

"Yes, sorry about that. He really likes you." He chuckles.

"Well, tell him I really like him, too, and I can't wait to meet him soon." She leans up and kisses Parker on the lips.

Parker captures her head in between his hands, not allowing her to escape the kiss she started. The kiss he'll end, when he's ready.

He pulls Addison up over him, his hands under her arms, as he lies back on the couch. She's lying on his body, chest to feet. He presses his knees together, having her legs fall to the outside of his, straddling him.

Parker keeps the kisses soft, sensual, hot. He admitted that he loved her, and she said it as well. He wants to explain to her about the mating and make sure she's comfortable with it. It's very sexually exciting and will continue to be after they're mated as a couple.

The first sexual encounter of the mating ritual is the connecting of the bond between him and Addison and he'll have to make sure she's good and ready for it. He's been through the mating but never a soul mate mating. He's not sure if it's the same, or more intense. And it sure isn't going to be on the couch.

Parker pulls his lips from Addison's, slowly, still nibbling and licking hers. Teasing her for what's more to come. Addison sits up, her over-heated core on top of his very hard, and very ready to go, erection.

"Addison, you're my soul mate and I'm not going to take you and make you my mate on this couch. Not tonight. But I will, soon. London can have her own room upstairs, when you're ready for her to. Then when you're ready, truly ready for me, I'll take you and make you mine. Forever." Parker says to her in a low, sensual voice, almost a growl. He pulls back a wayward strand of her hair and tucks it behind her ear. Letting his fingertips linger there around the shell of her ear.

Parker sits up more on the couch and he can hear his inner cat highly protest what he just told Addison. His cat wants to mate her now and is fighting with Parker to get out and do so.

Parker eases from underneath Addison and she looks confused by his moving away from her. "It's not you, honey. I have another voice telling me to do things to you and now is not the time." He smiles at her, easing the sting.

Parker checks the time and it's already after eleven. He pulls Addison off the couch and into his arms. Her arms wrap around his neck and she rests her head on his upper chest. He knows she can hear his heart beating, and a low purr resonating from it.

"You know, I thought I could hear that before but wasn't sure what it was. Now, I know. It's your cat. He's content with me, isn't he?"

"Oh, Addy. He's way more than content with you." He chuckles and then they shut off the lights, and he follows her to the master bedroom.

He shuts the door behind him and Addison checks on London in her crib. Her little diaper butt is in the air and she's asleep on her tummy. Addison rubs her back and then turns to Parker.

"She's something, isn't she? I don't know who or what I would be right now without her in my life. I love her so much, Parker."

"Yeah, Addy. She's something all right. She's a beautiful little girl. I just haven't figured out if she's a shifter yet. I can't scent anything. If Derek is a shifter, normally cubs don't shift until after their first birthday. When is it again? August, isn't it?" Parker inquires.

"Yes, her birthday is August first. Why?"

"She should have her first shift soon after if she has any shifter blood in her. So, I've been told, anywhere between twelve to eighteen months is when they have the first shift. When they're walking and running around, steady on their feet."

"I'm nervous and scared for that. To find out about that. What if Derek is a shifter? I ran from him. Do you think that maybe this is another reason he didn't want London, or any baby? He didn't want the responsibility of one?" Clearly Addison's brain is working now and fueling her questions.

"I'm not sure what he's thinking, Addy. And that's what has me on edge. I don't know what to expect from him. I do know he is going to come back."

"I'm not afraid of him anymore, Parker. I know you'll protect me from him. I'm waiting for him and I know we'll be ready when he does come for me. Because he'll have to go through you first." Addison's getting braver and Parker can see her true self, the one she's hidden away for so long, finally come out. And he likes what he sees in her.

After changing into pajamas, they both slip into bed and Parker pulls Addison closer to him. He turns her over and spoons behind her back.

He can tell she feels his hardness behind her when she wiggles just a bit. Parker's hand on her hip stops her and she giggles.

"Go to sleep, Addy. We have a big day tomorrow. I love you, babe. So much already." He sits up and kisses her temple then lies back down behind her.

"I love you, too, Parker. Goodnight."

Parker can feel Addy's body slip into slumber, and he holds her closer. He drifts off to sleep soon after.

Chapter Twelve

THE NEXT MORNING, Parker is up with the morning sun peeking over the horizon. He didn't sleep very well, knowing he was going to have to take a life, the life of Derek. Parker needs to protect them, though. Addison and London's life are in his hands.

He can scent Max and his bear family in the woods around his home and a few miles out. They lead up to the road, where he first saw Derek's truck parked and then they lead back to the house.

He knew he could count on Max. He's been a good friend over the years. Even after Hailey died, Max made sure they kept in contact.

Now, as Parker does a quick run in his leopard form, he can scent bear all around him. Not marking territory, just traveling through. He's glad he has his shifter friends to talk to.

He'd called Max early this morning and asked him to meet him in the woods, so Parker knew he'd be there. Quickly, he shifts into human form when he hears him coming closer.

"Max, it's me," Parker announces.

Max quickly shifts into his human form and they discuss the issue with Derek. Parker's concerns are if Derek is full human or shifter. The scent he's picked up could be shifter, but he could be hiding it, somehow.

"I can walk around town and see if I can scent him, flush him out if he's a true shifter. If he's human, then he just stinks." Max says.

Parker chuckles, wishing it was that easy. "He's never told or hinted to Addison that he was one. But, she's also never knew that shifters existed before I told her last night."

"You told her you're a leopard shifter, then? How'd she take that. and have you shown her yet?" Max asks cautiously.

"She was asking a lot of questions. She's a big reader and she's read shifter books before. So, she's read on some of the customs from that. As for showing her, no, I haven't shown her yet." Parker tells him.

"You plan on showing her soon?"

"Yeah, soon. Hopefully before that asshat comes back. I don't want to scare her if I have to shift quickly to protect her, ya know?"

"Yeah, I know. It would definitely scare her if she witnesses a man blowing up into a black leopard." Max chuckles.

"So, you have Derek's scent then, and you're going to try to track him down? I don't want to be gone from the house too long in case he comes sniffing around while I'm out running." Parker tells him.

"We got this, Parker. We'll get him. I'll check in with you in a few hours and let you know where he is. I already have two scouts in town looking for him." Max is confident in his scouts.

"Okay, thanks, Max. I knew I could count on you to help. You've been a good friend to me. I appreciate it."

Max and Parker give a quick man hug and back away from each other.

"We've been friends since we were cubs, man. I'll always be here for you, and I know you've got my back as well. I've got your hide on this one. We've got this. Relax and go snuggle with that woman of yours."

"Okay, but just let me finish him off." Parker lets out a low growl. "If it comes down to it, I might have your woman come meet with Addison, give her someone to talk to and distract her, if need be. It might be a good thing anyway."

"No problem. He's all yours. I'll text you in a few hours, man, and I'm sure Shannon would love to come meet and visit with your new mate to be." Max chuckles and shifts into his bear. Parker shifts into his leopard, and they both lumber back to Parker's home together.

Upon returning, with the sun still low in the morning sky, Parker shifts into his human form and Max, still in his bear, lumbers towards his own home to the west. With a nod to each other, they go their separate ways.

Parker enters the house, using his key, through the back door. He opens it with a soft click and shuts and locks it behind him. It's only about six in the morning, so he slips out of his clothes and into bed only wearing his boxers, snuggling up behind Addison's sleeping form.

An hour later and he's still awake. Addy flipped over when he first got into bed, throwing her arm and leg over his body and resting her head on his chest. Doesn't take much for this woman to give him an erection.

Knowing he can't do anything about it, London's in the room and will be waking up soon, he wills his cock to go down. *Down boy. Soon, very soon.*

You need to mate with her. Derek will be back to try to take her away. She won't be able to protect herself. His leopard is angry.

Calm down. Derek won't take her. And since when are you such a Debbie Downer suddenly?

You can see how Addy has changed. She's more her normal self, or what I would think would be her normal self. I like what I see every day. I'll mate with her when I think she's ready. This is all new to her. Parker tries to calm his cat.

I know. I just want her to be safe. His cat settles back down.

I know. I do too. Parker replies, snuggling into Addison and pulling her in tighter.

***

A few hours later, when breakfast has been consumed, dishes done, and London's morning bath is over from making a mess with syrup, Parker leads the girls into the woods on the trail.

"We won't go far, but it's a beautiful day out and I figured we could go for a walk." Parker says.

"Maybe we could buy a stroller for London until she gets bigger. Is the trail pretty good for one?" Addison asks.

"Most of it's even. We could go buy a stroller tomorrow morning and then come for a walk. I really want to show you my land. The wild animals, the flowers in the summertime, just the all-around beauty of nature around here."

"I bet it gives your leopard room to run." Addison looks to the ground and then peeks up to Parker as she asks.

Parker stops walking with London in his arms and pulls Addison closer to him in a tight embrace, kissing her lips. "Yes. It gives him plenty of running room." He chuckles, and they continue to walk, holding hands. He's enjoying the easiness that Addy has accepted him and his leopard.

A few times Parker sets London down and holds her hands in his, helping her walk. Letting her see things from her point of view.

On their way back, Parker can scent Max not too far from where they are, and he's concerned about Addison's reaction if he makes himself known. The wind shifts, and Parker can tell Max is leaving and is relieved that he didn't have to explain that one.

When they near the house, Parker stops, and smells the air. Just checking. Nothing different. Addison notices and asks him, concerned, "What's wrong, everything okay?"

"Yeah, just checking. All's clear. I wanted to let you know that I have some shifter friends out in the woods until we can get rid of Derek. They're helping patrol and they'll let me know if anything happens."

"Patrol?"

"Yes, checking to see where the as...ah...Donkey face is at." He smiles and catches his words before saying them in front of London.

"Okay, so now you have other people involved, Parker. I don't want them getting hurt, either." She expresses concern.

"Addy, listen to me. They're all shifters, too. I just wanted you to know in case you saw a few bears, wolves, or other animals around. Still, don't go out to them, it might be a wild animal, but I want you to know." Parker tells her, guiding his palm over her cheek.

"Okay, Parker. I'll be careful."

"Let's go get London a stroller now so I can take you back to the river and streams. It'll be easier for us to maneuver her around." Parkers excited about this idea.

"Sounds good to me."

They head back to the house and Addison goes in to grab London a bag and Parker buckles her into her car seat. Addy jumps in the truck a minute later.

When they arrive in town, Parker parks in the baby store lot and shuts off the truck. He turns to Addison and cups her cheek in his palm.

"I'm buying her the stroller today. No arguments, okay?" Parker tells her.

"Parker, you've bought everything for her so far. I can buy her things. I have my own money." Addy informs him.

"I know you do. But I like buying her things. I want to buy you things, too. Will you let me? I've noticed you're low on clothes and I want to make sure you have what you need."

Addison looks at Parker, gazing into his eyes, and breathes out, heavily. "Fine, if it'll make you happy." Not too happy herself.

He gets that she wants to be independent, on her own. Not wanting to depend on Parker like she was forced to with Derek. He chose to buy her what he thought she needed. She likes the care Parker has given her and London so far, but she needs to know that she's her own separate identity. She's her own woman.

"I need clothes. I only grabbed a few things I had to have. I grabbed most of London's things."

"Addy, is there anything at Derek's place that you would like to have back? I'm asking because after this is all over, we can go back and clear out the house and take what's yours and bring it back here." Parker suggests to her.

"Yes, I have a lot of things there I would like to get. I have personal things there. London has things there from her birth and growing up so far. Photos of her when she was a newborn baby. I even took pictures of me pregnant each month. Minus any bruises." Addison adds.

"Okay then, as soon as this is over, we're going there." Parker says sternly.

Parker grabs her hand, kissing the back of it then grabs the keys. He helps her down from the passenger side and then picks London out of her car seat.

Occasionally, he can smell a faint scent from London. Shifter? But it's so faint, he's not sure. It could just be because she's Derek's blood and she picked that up from him.

Hopefully, we'll find out soon. His leopard whispers.

Yes, very soon. Stop whatever you're doing, you're making me dizzy. Are you pacing? Parker asks.

If I would be able to pace, yes. Then I'm pacing. Sorry, I'll try to relax. The cat replies, and finally settles down.

***

Parker guides Addison and London into the baby store and they walk right over to the strollers. He shows Addy a stroller with three wheels. He's seen some women who run using these strollers. It has bigger wheels and looks to be lightweight but sturdy. An all-terrain stroller.

Addison agrees, and they buckle London in for a test drive. Parker zooms the little girl up and down a few isles of the store, jogging slowly. London is laughing and giggling in glee and clapping her hands together, kicking her feet.

They make the purchase and put it in the back of the truck bed, Parker locking it up. Next stop is a clothing store for Addison, and just maybe a few things for London since they are already out and about.

Addison looks around at the clothes and chooses jeans, shorts, socks, panties, a few bra's and shirts. She grabs a new purse as well. The one at Parker's is about to have a broken strap.

Parker pushes the cart with Addison's things and he walks them back to the baby department. Parker flips through the clothes, checking London's size tag on the inside of her tee shirt.

Addison goes and grabs another box of diapers and a container of wipes. Parker grabs a few outfits and then they look at shoes for her. Addison notices her own shoes and decides she could use a new pair of tennis shoes along with her clothing.

They find sandals and tennis shoes for London and Addison as well. When they have everything, and more, Parker pushes the cart up to the register to pay for everything.

After Parker pays, and Addison gets London safely buckled, Parker locks up the bed of the truck once again with their items safely inside.

Parker drives them to the diner for a late lunch, and he parks the truck. Walking inside and reading the sign saying, 'Please seat yourself,' they choose a booth and get London buckled in a high chair. Parker and Addison glance over the menus and the waitress sets down two glasses of water shortly after.

"Hi, my name is Katie. I'll be your server today. Do you need a few minutes to decide?" Katie talks in a younger teen voice. She looks to be around sixteen.

"If we could have a few minutes, thank you, Katie." Parker turns and tells her. Katie leaves with a quick nod and tends to another booth.

Parker and Addison look over their menus and order their lunch, and steamed carrots and a scrambled egg for London.

"Parker, um... I'm kind of curious...when do you think I can meet your cat?" She talks quietly and glances shyly up at Parker.

He smiles at her, knowing she must have more questions about this new world she's been told about.

"Soon, Addy. Soon. We can talk about this in a more private area later, okay?"

Addison nods in agreement as the waitress comes back to give them their lunch plates. As they eat their food. Her brain is on overload with the news of shifters in the world.

How many animals? What breeds? Are they all over the world living in secret like Parker and his friends? Do they work normal nine to five jobs, as well? Does it hurt to shift?

217

Parker had mentioned that he was concerned if Derek was a shifter. If he is, does that mean London is, too? What kind would she be and when would she shift? Parker mentioned at a year old. It's not that far away. The beginning of August is London's birthday and it's not that far away.

"Parker, when we get back home, could I use your phone and call my sister? I still haven't called her, and I would like to let her know London and I are safe." She asks.

"Sure, not a problem."

After their meal is eaten and the bill is paid, Parker buckles a sleepy London in her car seat and helps Addison into the big truck.

***

On the way home Parker's cell rings out into the cab of the truck. He pulls over and puts the truck in park. Pulling out his cell he glances at the caller and notices it's Max.

Here we go. Parker thinks.

I'm more than ready. The leopard answers back, growling.

"Hello, Max. What's up?" He casually asks. Not wanting to frighten Addison.

"Found him. He's parked on the north side of your property and he has supplies. He's hiding out in the old run-down hunting cabin about three miles from your house."

"We're on our way back now. The truck is full of things for Addison and London. Can you call your women and have them meet us at the house? Then Addison and London won't be alone. Is Derek alone?"

"As far as my scout can tell, yes, he's alone. But it seems like he's been here for some time. When Mike checked the cabin when Derek left, he found food and other supplies in the cabin, like he had been actually living there for a little while."

As Parker talks to Max on the phone, Addison can feel her anxiety amp up and her nerves are getting the best of her. Her breathing increases and she's getting light headed.

Parker must notice because he ends the call quickly. "Got to go Max, I'll see you soon." Parker sets the cell on the dash of the truck, "Addison, honey. Are you okay? Look at me, please."

Addison turns her head and looks at Parker's concern etched in his handsome face. "I'm okay, Parker. I heard your side of the call and I know that Derek's been found. The thought that he won't ever give up scares me."

"Addison, this ends today. After this is over, you won't ever have to worry about him again. Do you understand me? I love you, Addison. You and London both. I want you to be my mate, and London to be my daughter. I love you with everything that I am, including my leopard. When we find our mates, it's for forever, Addison. I want you to know that."

"I understand, Parker. Let's go home and finish this, once and for all. I don't want to be looking over my shoulder all the time, waiting for him to jump out from the bushes." She whimpers, and a few tears fall from her eyes.

Parker leans over and wipes them with his thumbs, then hugs her as close as the seatbelts will allow them.

"Let's get home. I have some ass kicking to do." Parker announces.

Addison smiles slightly, and then leans against her passenger door. Parker drives back onto the road, quickly pocketing his cell in his front jean pocket.

"I told Max to gather the women to keep you company. They are around your age and will help you with London." Parker tells Addison quietly.

She nods in agreement.

"It sounds like he's been camped out in the old hunting cabin a few miles from the main house. We're not going to wait for him, we're bringing the fight to him."

She nods again.

Parker grabs her cold hand in his and intertwines their fingers together. Her lighter skin against his tanned fingers.

As Parker drives down the long driveway, he makes out a few bears and wolves in the woods.

Only another shifter could see them with their keen eyesight. Addison just looks straight ahead.

"Addison, my shifter friends are all here. They're in the woods in their animal forms. Don't be afraid if they come out of the woods to greet us and give us the update. I know I haven't shown you or told you everything. I wanted to ease you into my world slowly, but I've run out of time. I'm sorry, I was hoping I would have more time to show you my shifter world." Parker blows out a frustrated breath.

Parker pulls up to the house and parks the truck, seeing that Max is sitting in one of the rockers on the front porch already. The front door opens and a pretty, black haired, short, kind of heavy woman walks out.

"That's Max, and his wife, Shannon. She's your age." Parker says.

"Okay. Parker, I'm scared. I'm shaking and I'm not sure how I feel." Addison's voice trembles.

Parker shuts off the truck and unbuckles his and Addison's seatbelt. He pulls her closer and sits her across his lap, holding her close. Both of her feet on the bench next to them.

"Addison, there's no need to worry. We'll take care of this." He whispers in her ear, kissing her there.

"I know." She ducks her head to hide her tears. Max and Shannon walk into the house, giving them the privacy they need.

"Come on. Let's get London inside and all your things. You can put everything away and when you're done, I'll be back."

Parker opens the door and slides out, setting her on her feet. He walks around and pulls London from her seat, and carefully hands her sleeping body to Addison.

She brings her daughter in the house and Max comes out, holding the door for Addison. Shannon meets her just inside the house and hugs her. Typical Shannon, she's a hugger.

The bears, now in human form, come out of the woods, five of them and they all approach Parker with their news. Max reaches him first and the men help with the unloading of the stroller and bags of items from the bed of the truck and bring it all inside the house.

It takes one trip to get everything inside and dropped off in the living room. The stroller is pushed into the laundry room by the back door.

***

Addison shuts the bedroom door after putting London in her crib, and she meets everyone in the kitchen. Soft spoken words lead her there, respectful of a sleeping baby.

When Addison enters the room, Parker, Shannon, and Max turn her way. The other men have left. Parker introduces everyone, and Addison acknowledges them, still dancing in a brain full of fog.

Max leaves and Shannon puts her arm around Addy, leading her to the living room. Parker hangs his head, both hands on the back of a kitchen chair. He's being forced to take a life.

Parker enters the living room and sees Addison sitting on the couch, Shannon next to her. Their talking in hushed voices. Parker walks over to Addy and pulls her up and into his arms, against his muscular chest.

He smiles down to her, "Addison, I've just found you. I'm not going to lose you. I love you and we're going to be soul mates very soon. I promise you." He smiles again and kisses her lips softly once more. "I'll see you soon." And with that, Parker leaves the house.

With Shannon here, the house still seems empty. London's asleep in her crib, which is still in the master bedroom. That should be moved soon to another room.

It sounds like when Parker says the mating thing, that's a forever promise. Like a marriage. Addison hopes so. She would love to be married to Parker. She truly loves him with all her heart. He proclaimed the same just minutes ago, in the truck.

Addison and Shannon talk a bit, but mostly she stays quiet and she listens to her talk. Shannon looks to the window, then to the back room occasionally. Guessing she can hear things Addison can't.

"Can you hear what's going on?" Addison finally asks Shannon, nervously.

"Yeah, sorry." She sheepishly says. "They're on their way back. They have Derek with them, alive and kicking." She gasps, "That man has a filthy mouth!" Shannon exclaims.

"You have no idea. He basically kept me as his personal punching bag and whore for the past year and a half or so."

"Oh, Addison, I'm sorry. I didn't know. Max just said you were with a demon monster that was cruel to you. I didn't hear anything else. I didn't know it was really like that." Shannon hugs Addison close. "I hope we can become good friends. Your London is the same age as our little Benny. He's already one, as of July fourth, just last week."

"How sweet. You didn't bring him?" Addison asks.

"I actually did. He's in Parker's bedroom upstairs sleeping. He'll sleep for another hour or two. My younger sister, Bethany, is up there with him. She'll watch over the kids if we need to go outside for any reason." The way Shannon says that it makes her think that she should be going outside. "I left the twins at home with friends. They're four, Gracie and Tanner."

"You have twins, too?"

Addison looks out the front window, nothing yet.

"Yup." She huffs out a breath. "The men will be coming up soon. Let's go meet them there, they're almost here now."

Addison and Shannon walk to the door, glancing outside. With Addison's human sight, she can't see anything, even though it's mid-afternoon.

"Oh, they've roughed him up a little bit, I see." Shannon quietly says.

Addison keeps looking where Shannon has her eyes trained and she still can't see anything. The tree line is around eighty feet from the house and she can't see anything but leaves and trees.

Shannon opens the screen door and walks outside, Addison following, cautiously.

Shannon bounces down the few steps it takes her to hit the ground and Addison clutches the railing on the deck with her fingers. She can hear them coming. Derek shouting and swearing about 'wanting to kill them' and them 'keeping his whore.'

Parker breaks through the tree line, finally, dragging Derek by the upper arm. He's walking but stumbling, because every step Parker takes, it's two for Derek. Seeing the two of them side by side, takes her breath away.

There's no comparison. Parker shines and is all male, raw power, muscle and sharp lines. Derek has rumpled clothing, unkempt hair, and an unshaven face.

These two men in her life are so very different. One is an ugly demon who tormented her every day of her life. The other one, her protector. An angel sent to heal her from the inside out. The one she'll be with for the rest of her life.

Chapter Thirteen

"ADDISON, YOU WHORE! Get your fat ass down here so I can take you home. How dare you come here and spread your legs for another man! You're *mine*, you bitch!" Derek screeches at her and Parker lets go of his arm.

Derek breaks into her moment of gazing at Parker.

"Fuck you, Derek. I was never yours to begin with." Addison finds herself face to face with the demon himself before she even realizes she's moved off the back porch. "Fuck. You!" She pokes him in the chest with each word.

Derek raises his right hand as if to strike Addison across the face. Addison's vision goes from bright colors to blazing red. She never feels the slap to her face from him. She screams, growls and hisses at Derek, "No! You're never going to hurt me again! You're never going to touch me again! You're never going to rape me again! You're never going to lay a fucking finger to touch me again! You're a piece of shit and don't deserve to live on this earth or hurt another person again."

She can feel her fingers claw across Derek's face and body, scratching, punching, and kicking him. Screaming and venting all her past hurt, anger, fear and anxiety onto this pitiful, sorry excuse of a man. All she sees is red behind her eyes. And her anger, fear and all the pent-up emotions come out of her in a rage against the man who tormented her all this time.

When Addison finally opens her eyes, not realizing she's closed them, she's lying on the ground, breathing heavily. Her face is down, looking at the dirt in front of her. She looks up to the people around her and Parker is crouched down in front of her, brushing her hair back from her tear-streaked face.

"Addison. Holy shit, sweetheart. Are you okay?" Parker's expression is in awe. He's scared for her. What did she do?

Addison goes to stand up from the dirty ground and she knows she's standing but is only waist high to Parker. What the hell?

She looks down to her feet and sees large paws. Very large, white and black striped tiger-like paws streaked in red. Blood. She takes a step forward, yup, they move when she wills them to move.

Holy Shit! Addison's a tiger shifter!

When Parker noticed Addison stepping from the back-porch steps, she was angry. She was yelling at him, poking her finger into his chest. When Derek went to slap her, she vibrated and shook her whole body. Not in fear. Not in anger. But in *shifting*.

Addison was shifting!

She shifted instantly, and her clothes shredded right from her body. One moment, she was a human woman in a rage, the next moment she was a big white tiger, pouncing on her prey, growling, snapping and clawing at his face and body.

All Parker, Max and Shannon could hear is Addison growling at Derek. And Derek's high pitched, shrill screaming. A man about to lose his life to a very pissed off lady tiger shifter. Parker knew she was yelling and screaming at him, but in her mind because she was already a tiger at that moment.

Addison sits on her back haunches, her body trembling over knowing the news that's she's a shifter. Her fear of being a shifter outweighing the fear of being around Derek right now.

Addison turns back and sees Derek, a bloody mess of flesh, and torn clothing. Gore to another human being caused by her own hands, or rather, claws.

He's still alive and breathing, barely. She can see his chest moving. She walks over to him, still in her tiger form, and lies down next to him on her stomach. She whispers in his ear when he turns to face her.

"I win, you motherfucker. I fucking win," is all Addison says to him as he lays there, bleeding out on the ground.

Parker watches Addison sit up, then stand on four trembling legs. She's in shock. Her body isn't used to this change and this fast.

Suddenly, Parker watches Derek, he moves to sit up and his right hand reaches out for Addison, still in her tiger form.

She must hear him gurgle from his mouth and throat because she whips around so fast, she's a blur and the next thing, she has Derek's neck in her mouth.

With a quick shake of her head, she bites down…

Snap!

Parker sees the life drain from the man's eyes, and Derek's arm falls from her shoulder, hitting the ground. She drops him like a bad habit from her mouth and takes a few steps back from his dead body, then collapses herself.

She's unconscious.

Parker rushes to her side and tries to lift Addison. She's much heavier in her tiger form and Max hurries over to help Parker bring her into the house.

Shannon reaches the door first and opens it for the two men, lugging in this huge tiger. Parker thinks she might even be bigger than him in his leopard form. They quietly bring her into the master bedroom. Knowing London is sleeping there but wanting Addison to be comfortable.

Parker, not seeing London in her crib, looks to Bethany, who has come from upstairs.

Bethany says to him, "I moved her upstairs earlier."

Parker nods his thanks, and Max and Parker lay Addy on the big bed.

Her small human frame, holding back this huge tiger from the world. She didn't even know shifters existed, and here, she is one! Her large tiger taking up most of the king size bed now.

Parker doesn't know of her family background except that she has a sister. But why wouldn't her sister tell her about it, and why would Addison shift now, and not when she was younger?

So many questions, and no complete answers. And they still have no idea if Derek was a shifter either, dammit! Parker was in shock himself as he watched the woman he loves shift into a massive white tiger. But then also to watch her attack Derek and shred him apart, that was totally a different reaction.

Derek was left outside bleeding on the dirt. The whole front of his body is unrecognizable. Addison ripped him apart. She had totally let the tiger take over her human emotions and he's afraid that when she wakes up, she will still be in the tiger form, and Addison left in the background, afraid and unsure of how to return.

He's trying to remember back when she started yelling at him, she was talking while in the tiger form, so maybe...maybe he'll be able to talk to her and get her to calm the tiger, so Addison can shift back to human. Her clothes ripped and shredded from her when she shifted, so those are gone. He knows she'll be naked when she shifts back to human.

He heard her with a gruff voice when she told Derek she had won. Her tiger can speak human, so that's a different turn of events. He's so damn proud of her for standing up to Derek, but now so terrified of the outcome.

"Parker, what do you want us to do with Derek?" Max asks quietly.

"Just get rid of him somewhere. He doesn't deserve to rot in peace six feet under. Let the animals feast on his sorry ass. At least he can benefit something good and they can fill their bellies." Parker replies, just as quietly.

"I'll let my scouts know. Deeper in the woods, the better I think, huh?" Max asks.

"They can drop him from the cliffs if they want. I don't fucking care."

"I'll be right back." Max turns to Shannon, who's been standing in the doorway. "Honey, can you and Bethany stay here and watch the cubs for us? I'm going to let the scouts know what to do."

"Sure thing, babe, I'll run up and check in on them now. They should be waking up soon." Shannon and Max hug intimately, kissing on the lips quickly, then going their separate ways.

Parker looks back to Addison, at her unconscious tiger form, and she's just purely an amazing being.

He pets the top of her massive head, down her neck, to her shoulder. Tiger fur. He's never met a tiger shifter before, let alone a white tiger. They are one of the very top of the cat line. Regal.

Addison growls low and deep in her throat, a soft purr and Parker chuckles quietly. Thinking back to when Addison laughed at his cat purring with her in his arms.

Parker gets up and grabs comfy clothes for Addison, she'll need them and a shower when she wakes, and sets them on the counter by the bathroom sink.

Parker sits back on the bed, pushes himself against the headboard and strokes Addison's massive head again.

She needs to wake up soon. I can't believe this. A white tiger shifter! Why didn't we scent this before? Parker's leopard decides to break the silence.

She'll wake when her body is ready to. For now, we wait. London is cared for, we just need to wait for Addison, and I'd wait forever for her. She shifted really fast and not knowing what she truly was, her body and mind are in shock.

I agree. She is our one true soul mate. We'll wait for her to be ready and come back to us. Parker's cat purrs, settles down and is silent once again.

An hour and a half later, London and Ben are awake and playing with her toys in the living room. They're eating a snack of crackers and sharing with each other, feeding each other.

Max and Parker carefully bring London's crib up to Parker's old room. Bethany and Shannon bring up the baby clothes, diapers, and other things to make the new bedroom complete.

Parker unpacks Addy's things from her suitcase, finally. She is home and forever Parker's. She's not going to be leaving anytime soon. With her suitcase safely stashed in the closet and her personal things put away, he eases back into bed with Addison.

Knowing the kids are taken care of, he leans over to Addison's furry ear, "Sweetheart, you need to wake up. We need to go over a few things."

That's an understatement. His leopard chuffs.

I know. But if she doesn't wake up soon, I'm going to worry more about her. She should have woken up by now and I'm eager to talk to her about all this. Parker tells his leopard.

Me too. I can feel her tiger yet, so Addison still is hanging back. Talk to her, Parker, get her to hear you, or she'll wake up as the tiger and not human.

"Babe, Addy, you need to wake up. Come on, London needs you. I need you to wake up." Parker says softly.

Addison groans and lightly growls at the intrusion of sleep. She slowly opens her eyes as Parker gently shakes her shoulder. Her light blue eyes appearing from under the lids.

"Good afternoon, sleepy head." Parker smiles at her. Seeing her eyes and knowing she sees clearly who he is.

"Ummm." is all she says. Almost a growl.

Parker coaxes her, "Addy, I need you to think of your human body. The way your legs feel, your arms, your back. Feel them stretching and then do that with your body, baby. I need you to come back to me."

She stretches out on her belly, stretching out her front legs, her back legs, completely taking over the bed. Her front paws flop over the edge when she runs out of room. She yawns and her enlarged teeth all on display.

Parker can see her body tremble, and slowly her human body returns, her bones realigning to make her human once again.

Parker notices the surprise on her face, "Yeah, you were a tiger." He chuckles.

"Holy shit, Parker. I'm a tiger shifter?"

Parker pulls her back to him and lifts the blankets to cover her up. He chuckles, "Yeah. You're a tiger shifter. I'm guessing you never knew."

"I had no idea shifters even existed until you told me, let alone me even being one!" She's clearly upset, and a tear falls down her cheek.

"Hey now, it's okay. We'll figure it out. I do have some questions though, about your family."

"I never knew my parents. I was adopted and lived with them since I've been little. I have one sister and I had a brother, but he died when we were young. He had leukemia." Addison explains.

Parker says, "I'm sorry about your brother, Addison. What about your sister, I know you should call her, but was she adopted, too? Are you adopted sisters or are you blood sisters?"

"Yes, all three of us were adopted. I doubt she's a shifter, or I would have known about it. We told each other everything. When I went with Derek, she encouraged it. He wasn't evil back then. He just slowly made excuses for me not to be close to her. Pulled at our relationship, until we barely spoke to each other but once every couple of months."

"Let's get you into the shower, you have dirt and dried blood on you. We'll talk more in there. I want to take care of you now."

He lifts her from the bed after pulling the blankets away, her body so much smaller now, and chuckles as he lifts her easily into his arms, against his chest. He rests his chin atop her head and walks to the bathroom. He sets her down on the edge of the tub and starts the water.

"You get in when it's warm enough. I'm going to let Max and the women know you're awake and that we're going to bathe." He kisses her lips quickly and leaves the room, shutting the door behind him.

Parker leaves Addy in the bathroom and quickly enters the living room, where Max is on the floor playing blocks with the two little ones. Bethany and Shannon are watching television quietly on the couch.

"I heard her talking. Crazy story, man. Just crazy." Max says as Parker walks over to him.

"I don't understand it either, but it is what it is. She wasn't with a shifter family, she's adopted. It sounds like she's been with them since she was a baby, too." Parker tells them. All eyes in the room are on him now.

"Maybe her birth parents were killed. As shifter parents, you would die to keep your cubs safe. Maybe something like that happened. Shifter parents don't just give up their cubs. We can't. It's in our nature to protect them. Not give them away." Max makes a point.

"Maybe her parents were killed or taken away. We may never find out." Parker bends down and kisses London on the top of her head then ruffles Ben's hair.

"I'm going to help Addison wash up. She has blood and dirt all over and she's still pretty shaken up. You guys okay with watching London a bit longer?" Parker asks his friends.

"She's not a problem. You go comfort and wash your mate. We'll be here if you need us." Max says.

"Thanks. We'll be out soon then we can go out to the diner for dinner. My treat. Your scouts, too." Parker announces.

"Good deal! We'll be waiting." Replies Max.

Parker makes it back in to the bathroom and Addison's already relaxing back in the hot water. She opens her eyes as he shuts the bathroom door behind him and begins to strip off his clothing. He eases into the water behind Addy and leans forward to shut off the water.

He grabs some body wash from behind him and the sponge, squirting some of the scented gel and plunging it into the water quickly, making some bubbles.

He begins to wash Addison's back, neck and wherever his hands can reach. He reaches around to the front and she leans against his chest. Parker washes her stomach, breasts, and shoulders as well.

Nothing sexual, even though he can feel himself poking Addy in the back. "Sorry about that." He chuckles as she smiles up at him. "My body has other things in mind for us. This time, right here, isn't about making love to you, Addy. This is about comforting you and making sure your mind can wrap around what happened."

"I know. I'm trying. It's weird now. I have a real voice in my head." She giggles and Parker chuckles at her statement.

"I don't understand why you haven't shifted before. This is your first time, and you're well overdue. Have you any idea who your birth parents are? Or their names?"

"My adoptive mom and I have looked and researched but never found anything. My birth certificate has my name, birth date and place of birth. The names on the certificate for parents are smudged so bad it's not readable. They must not want to be found." She sniffles at the thought.

"It's unusual for shifter parents to put a child up for adoption, unless they were killed, and no other family was around. I do know that the tiger shifters are rare and white ones are more rare. I've never met one, until now." He smiles and pokes her gently in the ribs.

Parker continues to wash Addy's body and they both wash and scrub her fingers clean. He drains the water and fills it back up again.

"You have to wash your hair, there's some blood in it." Parker says.

Addison slides forward, leans back and dunks her head under the water in front of him, her long hair swirling around his cock, caressing it with every movement.

She sits back up, wiping the water from her face with her hands. Parker grabs the shampoo and lathers it in her hair for her. She dunks again, letting Parker swirl her hair, making sure the soap is out. She sits up again and they do the same thing with the conditioner.

When she's finally clean and bubbles are out of her hair, he leans forward and kisses her shoulder and neck and just behind her ear. He lets the water out of the tub and stands up. He steps out of the tub and grabs a fluffy towel for each of them.

He helps her out of the tub and they each dry themselves off. He wraps the towel around his waist and walks into the bedroom, grabbing some clean clothes.

Addison dries off and notices her clean clothes on the counter by the sink and gets dressed.

Parker walks into the bathroom, where Addison is finishing up, and says, "I'm going to let Max and the women know we're ready to go."

She nods, and he walks out.

Upon returning, Parker has London in his arms and Addison smiles so big, it brightens her face. She quickly changes London's diaper and clothes and they jump in the truck, headed for the diner.

Parker reaches for Addy's hand, resting on the seat and he entwines their fingers together.

Addison and Parker don't talk about the elephant in the truck cab, Derek, and what was done with his body. They both leave it alone, for the time being, but Addison will want to know.

"Parker, can I use your cell to call my sister now? I keep forgetting."

"Yes, by all means. I'll get you your own cell, too." He hands over his cell and Addison punches in the number to her sister.

She leaves a message after the beep. "Hey, Ness, it's Addy. Um, I just want you to know that

London and I are safe. I got away from Derek and he won't be bothering us anymore. This number is good for you to call me back at until I get my own cell. Okay, well, I love you! Bye!"

With that call out of the way, Addison feels better that she at least contacted her sister. She puts the cell on the seat and slides her hand over to grab Parker's and links their fingers together.

"Parker, can I ask you a question?"

"Addy, you can ask me anything, anytime. You don't have to ask me if you can ask me something."

"Okay, then… Umm… What happened to me? How did I change and what did I do to Derek?"

"Well, you were on the porch when we brought Derek into the clearing and when he spouted off to you, well, it was like you moved so fast and then you were in his face. You yelled at him and poked him in the chest with your finger. It looked like he was going to backhand you, but…it was almost like you sensed it? I don't really understand it. You shifted right there on the spot and attacked him. Scratching, punching, and kicking with your tiger body. It was an amazing thing to watch, actually."

"Umm... All I remember is I was on the porch, then I was poking him. I don't remember how I got there. Just that I wasn't, then I was. He said bad things and I got very angry and all I saw was red. I could see him, but it's like I was wearing red-tinted sunglasses. I've never experienced anything like that before. When I realized he was on the ground, it was like all my strength disappeared. I felt him reaching towards me and I reacted. My human would never grab someone by the throat, but my tiger did. She killed him. Oh my God! I killed Derek!"

Parker quickly pulls over to the side of the road and slams the truck in park. He unbuckles both seat belts and pulls Addison onto his lap, cradling her head and her body into his. She's crying, and her body is trembling.

"It's okay, Addy. I've got you. I've got you, babe. Your tiger was protecting you and killed Derek. I can teach you to shift slower so it's easier."

"My whole body is sore. Like I've been stretched out and someone tried to piece me back together again. My muscles, tendons and my bones just...ache. Deep inside, too. Is this normal?"

"Addison, nothing about what you did was normal. We had no idea you were a shifter. And, usually, when we shift for the first time we're babies or toddlers. You're a full-grown woman. You shifted quickly and didn't give your human body the time to react. Your tiger reacted and came out to protect you. When we get home, if you're feeling okay, I'll show you how to shift, slowly. I think we need to wait a few days to let your body get back to normal, though. It will hurt to shift until your body gets used to the movements. Are you okay now? We can go back home, if you want." Parker's concerned, and he has every right to. His future wife went through a traumatic thing in her life.

"No, Parker, were not going to cancel on your friends for dinner and I think we need to wait a few days for the ache to go away before I shift again, too." Addison tells Parker, quietly.

Parker lets her go and she scoots back to her seat, buckling back in. Parker buckles up again, checks London, then steers back onto the road.

A few minutes later, he parks the truck in the diner's parking lot and they make their way inside. Parker notices Max and the others at a large table and two empty seats and an extra high chair for London waiting for them.

They all shake hands, hug one another, and he straps London in her seat, next to little Benny. They both giggle and grab each other's hands.

The waitress comes and takes everyone's orders. Returning with drinks on a tray, she makes another trip back later with the food.

"I just want to thank all of you for your help today with the issue we had, and any questions will be answered in time. This right here, is a thank you for your assistance today." Parker announces and spreads his hands out over the tables of food.

Parker sits and starts to eat, with everyone else in quiet conversation around him. He takes his left hand, sliding it over Addison's thigh and squeezes it. She looks down to his hand, then up to Parker's face. Seeing love, happiness, and contentment.

He leans over and kisses her quickly on the lips. "You make me happy, Addison." He grabs her hand in his and kisses her knuckles.

She smiles at him, "You make me happy, too, Parker." They smile again, and London squeals out loud, clapping her hands.

After dinner and with the check paid, Max and his family leave. Parker shakes hands with the scouts and tells them 'thank you' once again. After they leave, Addison, London and Parker leave for home.

When they arrive at home, Parker helps Addison out of the truck, and then grabs London from her car seat. Her birthday is right around the corner. He's wondering if Derek was a shifter, will London become a tiger shifter or become whatever Derek was? Only time will tell.

Chapter Fourteen

OVER THE NEXT week, Parker leaves Addison alone. No sexual advances. He wants her human to not be sore and he wants her ready, because the next time they make love, he's bonding them.

"Addison? I want to discuss something with you. We talked briefly of the mating bond and I want to make sure you want this." Parker begins.

"Parker, I want to talk to you, too. Give me a moment to get London down for her nap. I'll meet you in the living room." He nods, and she walks upstairs with a sleepy London.

A few minutes later, Addison enters the living room, and sits on the couch with Parker. "Okay, I want to know what your thoughts are." Parker asks.

"Parker. I've been with you for a while now and I know what I want. My tiger is pushing me." She laughs quietly.

"What do you want?" He's hoping it's him. He knows it's him. There's no mistake on what his leopard wants. They both want Addison for their wife, soul mate, forever. He loves her with all that he is, leopard and human.

"I want you, Parker. I've wanted you since I woke up that first day. I just never realized that it could be so intense. That there could be such a pull to you."

"That's your tiger." He chuckles. "I've been dealing with that same thing with my leopard since I saw you in the damaged car. I want you, too, Addison. Forever. If you'll have me?"

Parker presents a small black velvet box from his pocket and opens it, showing Addison the ring. "Will you marry me, Addison?"

She gasps, holding her hands over her mouth, and the tears begin to fall. "Parker. Yes. Yes, I'll marry you!"

They both reach for each other and embrace. Parker's leopard is purring, Addison's tiger is purring, and they can feel each other vibrate through their chests.

They let go and laugh because they know the animals inside are content as well with the decision Parker and Addison just made.

"Can I take you to bed now, Addy? I want to make love with you. I want to mate with you. I've waited to make sure your human body was no longer sore from shifting. Because after we mate, you're going to be sore all over again." He grins mischievously at her.

"Yes, Parker. I want to make love with you. Take me to bed, and let's become soul mates. I'm more than ready." Her breathing is heavy already, knowing what's to come.

Parker pushes the engagement ring on Addison's left ring finger. A perfect fit for this sparkly, round, one carat diamond. He has in mind what kind of set he wants for her, but that will come later. His cat is eager to mate and is sending images of Parker and Addison in the middle of passion.

Parker growls low in his chest, and Addison looks at him.

She growls back in a teasing way.

He picks her up, carries her to the master bedroom and shuts the door behind them. Gently he sets her on the bed, and she scoots back, lying her head on the pillow.

Parker crawls up and over Addison, straddling her thighs, then pressing one of his knees between hers. Slowly spreading her legs, still fully dressed, he lowers his body next to hers, kissing her lips.

Slowly they take off each other's clothing, dropping the articles onto the floor next to the bed. Now, both of them fully naked, Addison opens her legs fully, seating Parker, nestled where he finally wants to be. Fully erect and ready to claim his woman as his mate.

As Parker uses his fingers to slide to her wet opening, her hot center, just waiting for him. He pushes in one finger, making sure she's ready.

Oh, she's so ready for him. Parker removes his hand and grabs both of Addison's hands, linking their fingers together, and puts them above her head.

"Are you okay with this? Our hands like this?" Parker questions her. It's a form of dominance, and he wants to make sure it won't trigger anything with her.

"This is so good, Parker. I just need you to fill me. Hurry, I can't wait much longer." Addison's breathing is labored, and her eyes are glowing already. Her tiger is at the surface, waiting to mate as well.

He plunges his hot, aching cock into her. They both shout out and he holds her hands above her head. He gets better leverage as gets up on his knees and pumps into her, wildly.

The room is lightened by the light of day, but both of their eyes are glowing, leopard and tiger, Addison and Parker, relishing in the mating bond of lovemaking.

Parker lets go of Addison's hands and wraps his arms under her ribs, lying on top of her, her arms wrapping around his ribs, holding tighter, every tilt and movement he makes inside of her.

"Addison, you ready, baby? I'm making you mine, right now." He huffs and puffs from the overexertion of this mating with Addison.

"Yes, Parker! Make me yours!" Her legs wrap around his hips tighter and pulls Parker into her center further and she growls. Her claws are extending a bit, feeling her tiger close to the surface, her body about to shudder with her orgasm. So close, just a bit more.

Parker can feel that she's close, the fluttering in her muscles inside, deep inside. Wrapping around him like a warm, wet cushion.

Parker lifts up, looking down onto her, she releases her orgasm and screams out, "Ahhhh! Parker, now!"

Parker's canines elongate, and he bites down on her shoulder muscle, between her shoulder and her neck. Addison comes again, and he can feel his groin all wet. She's squirted. His hips still pumping out his orgasm into her warm wet core.

He lets go of her neck as he feels his teeth retracting back to normal human canines. He licks over the wounds, sealing them shut. Addison screams again and her canines bite down on Parker, on the same muscle, as he did to her and she comes again. This time, she has claimed him as her mate and the reaction from her makes Parker come harder than ever.

They both shout out their long-lasting orgasms and slowly come back down to earth, together. Parker leans to the side and lies down next to Addison, pulling her on top of him.

Her head resting on his shoulder. Her arm and leg are thrown over top him. They lay there, breathing heavily.

Parker's bite from Addison is already healing. And he notices her bite from him is sealed, but it will always leave a mark. Showing the mating bond. He looks down at her. Her body has a slight glow, all over. The magic is flowing through her.

She doesn't seem uncomfortable, so her body must be accepting his powers. Her tiger already has the healing and slow aging, but why would her body be glowing?

"Addison, are you okay?" Parker asks cautiously.

"Umm, hmm. Just sleepy." She mumbles back, then her breathing evens out and he knows she's asleep. Her body still in a soft yellow glow.

He can hear London upstairs starting to wake up, so he quickly and carefully removes himself from under Addison, without waking her. He grabs his underwear and puts them on and then covers Addy with the blanket. She doesn't move.

Parker runs up the stairs to the second floor and opens the door to London's room. She's standing up and looking out her window next to her bed.

"Hey there, pretty girl. Did you have a good sleep? Let's get you up and changed. Mommy will be awake soon." Parker gets her out and changes her diaper. Bringing her down to the main level, he puts her in the living room with her toys, then quickly enters the bedroom to get his jeans.

Addison is no longer glowing but is starting to stir. She's waking up, too. Parker pulls on his jeans. He sits on the bed next to Addison, "London just woke up a few minutes ago. I changed her and she's playing in the living room."

Addison stretches, and Parker can hear her bones crack in a few places. "Oh, I needed that." Addison laughs.

Parker kisses her on her forehead and tells her to come out when she's ready. She nods and then he leaves the room, not wanting London to be alone for too long.

When Parker walks into the living room, London is lying on the floor, her eyes shut and quietly still. Like she's asleep. He rushes over and feels for a fever, a sure sign of the first shift. She's warm, and so still. "London, honey. Wake up."

Addison comes out of the bedroom, hair brushed out and in a long ponytail, shorts, a cami top, and barefoot. She eyes London on the floor and runs over to her, trying to pick her up. Parker holds her arms back, whispering to Addison, "Let her be, Addy. And watch. She's going to shift soon."

"Parker, you said a year to eighteen months for their first shift! It's too early for her." Knowing that her first birthday is in two days, Addison and Parker sit cross-legged on the floor with London lying in front of them.

London's little body glows brighter and starts to tremble. She keeps her eyes closed and she is quiet. Her little body rolls over to her stomach and Addison gasps at the movement.

Parker holds Addy close and tries to soothe her with reassuring words.

London's little butt goes up in the air, her arms stretching out in front of her. She yawns big and loud, a small growl coming from her chest.

The tremors get more and more faster, almost making London a blurry mess on the floor. Her color changes and her clothes disappear. The tremors slow and what's left in London's wake, is an orange baby tiger.

Derek was human after all.

London opens her eyes and yawns again, her little growl coming out to greet Parker and Addison both.

Parker picks up London under his arm, he stands up and holds out his other hand for Addison. She takes it and he helps her up.

They make their way outside the back door, and to the forest. Parker in jeans and barefoot. Addison follows Parker into the woods about fifty feet and he sets London down on the dirt ground.

"London, look at me sweetie. I want you to be a good girl and sit here for a moment, can you do that for me?" Parker asks of the little tiger in front of him.

She nods and sits back on her haunches, then lies down, her head resting on her front paws. Parker turns to Addison, "Watch me shift, then you do the same. Think of your tiger. Your arms, legs and body becoming your tiger. It might hurt."

Parker stands back from them both, giving himself room. His body tremors and turns blurry, the next second, there's a baby tiger and a black leopard in front of Addison. Her turn.

She closes her eyes and pictures the tiger she became. She can feel her body tremble and shake, knowing her body is shifting. There's no pain, but the need to stretch is there. She follows that feeling and opens her eyes. She's eye to eye with the leopard but about a head taller. She's a tiger.

Can you hear me, Addison? Parker tries to make a mental connection.

Yes! Oh, my God! How are you doing that? Addison answers him in her mind.

Were mated. We can connect through our minds. London should be able to hear us as well. When she's able to talk, she'll be able to respond to us this way. Parker explains.

Come on, I want to show you the river. We can let the cats play. He chuckles and then he begins to lead them deeper into the forest.

After an hour of playing in the water and frolicking in the woods, Parker leads his family back to the house. All three of them are now resting on the back porch. He looks to London and Addison. *Think of your human form. Let it take over and stretch out.*

Addison closes her eyes, the tremors and the extreme feeling of stretching out overcomes her. She goes with it and when she opens her eyes, Parker and London are in their human form again. They stand up and enter the house.

Later on, Parker calls Max and asks him, "Have you ever heard of when a human turns into their shifter form for the first time that they glow?"

"Who's glowing?" Max asks with concern.

Parker answers back, "Both Addison and London are. London actually shifted early. Her year birthday isn't for a few days and when Addison and I finished the mating bond, she glowed. When she shifted earlier and we all went for our run, she glowed again before she shifted."

"Holy shit, Parker. If they glow after the bond and when they shift, damn. I've heard of it, but I've never seen it happen. It's only been talk. And Addison's a tiger shifter, so it could be...." Max is quiet for a minute, then continues, "Parker,

Addison's royalty. In the shifter world, there's a royalty line of tigers. I didn't know if they really existed. I thought they were wiped out or living elsewhere."

"Holy shit, Max. Are you sure?"

"Yes, I'm positive. Have you found out who her parents are yet?" Max questions.

"No. And I don't think we will ever find out. The writing of the parents listed on her birth certificate is so worn and rubbed off. Maybe it was done like that to put her into hiding. Maybe that's why she was put up for adoption."

"Wow, man. How does it feel to be linked to royalty?" He chuckles.

"Max, I don't care if she's royalty or some bum off the street. I love her. And now London's my daughter. Thanks, Max. We'll be in touch."

Parker walks into the living room and sits next to Addison on the couch. London's playing with her blocks and books.

"I heard what you said to Max. Sorry to eavesdrop. I can hear everything now. Everything is heightened." Addison looks to Parker, ashamed of hearing the private conversation.

Parker chuckles and pulls her in for a hug. "It's okay, Addy. I no longer have any secrets from you. I'm yours forever. London and I should make the bond. It's painless. It just means she's now my daughter. Like I'm adopting her. Is that okay with you?"

"What do you have to do to bond with her?" Addison questions and looks a little concerned.

"I have to exchange blood with her. She's a tough little girl and I know she'll be fine." Parker explains to her.

"Okay then. Can we do this now?"

"Yes. Give me a minute." Parker replies.

He closes his eyes and his body trembles a bit, he opens his eyes and they're glowing, his canines elongate. London stands up, and on shaky legs, walks over to Parker, like she knows what to do and expect.

She holds out her arms and he picks her up, setting her on his lap. He bites his wrist, and London does the same to her wrist, her eyes glowing and her teeth elongated as well. Parker and London lay their wrists on each other, blood slides together. When the blood from London touches the blood from Parker, it glows.

They both take a gasp and the glow dies off. They both lick the small wounds closed. London slides off Parker's lap and onto the floor, resuming her play like nothing ever happened.

I love you, Addison. Parker sends to her through his mind.

"I hope you know that. I love you with everything that I am, Addison. And now we're soul mates. London is now my daughter. Does this make you happy?" Parker leans back into the couch, pulling Addison with him.

Yes, I'm happy. I love you too, Parker, Addison says in her mind. "With everything that I am as well. I love you so much. And I'm happy it was you who found London and me. I'm truly happy here in your arms."

Parker and Addison kiss gently, pouring their everlasting love into this kiss.

"Dada."

Parker and Addison both break the kiss of everlasting love and look at London.

She's standing there, looking at Addison, then back to Parker.

"Dada." She points at Parker. "Momma", she points at Addison. London's first words.

Parker jumps up, grabs London in his hands and tosses her in the air. "Yes, little girl, I'm your daddy! Waa hoo!"

Parker is extremely excited that London is talking. She's made her first shift. Addison made her transition from human to tiger easily. London is a thriving, growing little girl.

Parker eases back into the couch, letting London play with her toys again. "I'm the happiest I've ever been. I have a family!"

Addison looks down to her hands tangled with Parker's fingers. "Parker, listen. Listen closely." Parker looks confused.

"What do you hear, Addison?" He asks.

"Be quiet. Listen very closely. You can just hear it. A faint thumping." Addison whispers.

Parker sits quietly next to Addison, eyes closed focusing his hearing. "I hear it now. Oh wow, Addison. Thank you!" He rests his hand over the lower part of Addison's stomach. The thumping is the start of a new life. Created by the love of Addison and Parker together.

Now, they can truly be a family.

THE END

About The Author

Noelle currently lives in Northern Minnesota with her husband, their four children, two dogs, a few pet rats, a handful of goldfish, and a very spoiled cat. She spends most of her days puttering away on the keyboard with a breathtaking view of a lake in her backyard as a source of tranquil inspiration. She and her husband were high school sweethearts, and celebrated their 25th year of wedded bliss in August of 2017. She enjoys fishing, reading, shopping, writing, and spending time with her family.

Noelle's writing career debuted as an indie author publishing her 'In Pieces', Book One, in the "Pieces Trilogy", a heterosexual contemporary romance. She also has released book 2, 'Shattered Pieces' and book 3 'Broken Pieces'. She originally published 'In Pieces' in 2015. The she wrote her first m/m romance, 'Returning for Ryder', in September 2016 with a publisher. Originally intended as a standalone novel, it seems Noelle's fans had other ideas and she penned a second, called 'Taking a Chance' and a third, 'Keelin's Return', in what is now 'The Returning Series'.

Naughty Night Press LLC signed Noelle for her MF Shifter Paranormal Romance, 'Remote in the Shadows', released in April of 2017. And released her YA/college love triangle themed new book, 'Lies' in January, 2018.

Noelle not only thrives on her love of writing, weaving worlds full of passion and romance for her readers to crawl into, but also the excitement of her readers when they know she's getting close to another release date. She plans to release many more books in the coming years for their enjoyment.

Be warned, no matter the genre of her work, Noelle's books will all contain explicit language and smexy romance scenes! 18+ audiences only!

Keep up with Noelle on Social Media

Amazon Author Page:

https://www.amazon.com/Noelle-Rahn-Johnson/e/B00ZZ0A226/

Official Facebook Author Page:

https://www.facebook.com/AuthorNoelleRahnJohnson/

Twitter: https://twitter.com/noelle_rahn

Blog: http://noellerahn-johnson.blogspot.com/

Signup for her Newsletter:

http://bit.ly/NoelleNL

Made in the USA
Columbia, SC
07 October 2018